SHIELDING MAYA

A SMALL-TOWN, ROMANTIC SUSPENSE NOVEL

GHOST LEGACY
BOOK 6

PJ FIALA

RT
ROLLING
THUNDER

DEDICATION

I've had so many wonderful people come into my life and I want you all to know how much I appreciate it. From each and every reader who takes the time out of their days to read my stories and leave reviews, thank you.
My beautiful, smart and fun Road Queens, who play games with me, post fun memes, keep the conversation rolling and help me create these captivating characters, places, businesses and more. Thank you ladies for your ideas, support and love.
The following characters and places were created by:

Reader who named Character -Name -Description
Debbie Bonsteel - Adam Jacobs - Zara Jacob's husband, Marni's father
Judy Hamilton - April - One of the women who saw the senator
Kristi Hombs Kopydlowski - Elsie - One of the women who saw the senator
Nathalie Juergensen - Zara Jacobs - Marni's mother, Adam's wife

Christa Stigler - Marni Jacobs - Young girl who lives in Hickory Hills. Befriended by Maya.

Last but not least, my family for the love and sacrifices they have made and continue to make to help me achieve this dream, especially my husband and best friend, Gene. Words can never express how much you mean to me.
To our veterans and current serving members of our armed forces, police and fire departments, thank you ladies and gentlemen for your hard work and sacrifices; it's with gratitude and thankfulness that I mention you in this forward.

DESCRIPTION

G HOST: Government Hidden Ops Specialty Team. They

She's a tough as nails GHOST operative.
He's next in line to lead his people into the future.
Life turns deadly for both of them after they witness a murder.

Maya Sager is far from being a girlie girl. She grew up preferring combat boots and tactical gear to shiny shoes and frilly dresses, much to her proper grandmother's chagrin. Maya loved and admired her mama and daddy, and wanted to follow in their honorable footsteps. Moving to Glen Hollow, Kentucky with her family of GHOST operatives gave Maya the chance to make her parents proud while fulfilling her childhood dream. Then she witnesses something she shouldn't and her world is turned upside down.

Jasiah Weston was born and raised on the Hill overlooking Glen Hollow, Kentucky. With his father on his deathbed, Jasiah is next in line to be President of his people. To solidify his place as leader, he must guide them through a peaceful merger with the residents of the small town below. When he and a tough yet gorgeous, GHOST operative towny, witness a murder, they are targeted for death.

Jasiah is determined to peacefully resolve old conflicts and bring the two towns together. But can he succeed while Shielding Maya from hostile factions with enough power to destroy the United States?

***

Entire series complete!

USA Today bestselling author PJ Fiala brings you the GHOST Legacy series—heroes willing to sacrifice everything in service to their country, and for the women they love. Full length novel with no cliffhanger, no cheating, and a happily-ever-after guaranteed.

... Sophie Vick ... Jute is a recon ... and runs the GHOST satellite office.

Aidyn Dunbar - Is the son of Bridget and Axel Dunbar. You can find their story is Defending Bridget. Aidyn's ...

Spencer Lawson - Spencer is the son of Wyatt and Yvette Lawson. You can read their story in Defending Yvette. Spencer specialize's in security, recon and recovery.

Henry Delany - Henry is the son of Hawk and Roxanne Delany. Their story is told is Defending Roxanne. His specialties are recon, recovery, and anything that requires size.

Adelaide Masters - Adelaide's parents are Josh and Isabella Masters. Their story is told in Defending Isabella. Adelaide served in the Army and is the team's medic.

Maya Sager - Maya served in the US Marine Corps. Her

parents are Dodge and Jax Sager. Their story is told in Finding His Jewel. Maya's specialty is recon and rescue.

Myles Sager - Myles served in the US Marine Corps. Myles and Maya are the twins of Dodge and Jax Sager. Myles is an explosives expert.

1

years.
up to him.
catching up with those he thought
impress. Now was the time it caught up to him. Now
was his time.

A branch slashed his right cheek. He grunted but
stalking
him moved toward him at a steady, even pace. His composure was scarier than the gun in his hand.

Tripping over a downed log, the senator fell with a thud in the heavy undergrowth. The smell of wet earth and decomposing leaves threatened to suffocate him. Rolling to his right side, he reached for the trunk of a small tree and pulled himself up. That's when the footsteps behind him stopped. The birds stopped chirping, the bugs even stopped their flight, and the utter silence around him made his heartbeat increase to a painful tempo. He should have stayed at the GHOST compound where he was safe instead of thinking he'd be able to get to his family.

Slowly turning his head to face his stalker, his eyes rounded when he saw the man standing before him. His hands at his sides, one still held a pistol, one hung free. He raised the pistol and shot once. The burning pain of the bullet as it entered his chest was dulled by his heart cramping and trying to beat. Still on his knees, he gasped.

"I didn't know you were involved," he huffed.

"You do now. Where's the recording?"

The senator hesitated. He'd set this whole thing in motion, he'd not stop it now. "It's with someone who is making changes."

The man shot once more, the echo of a gunshot rang out and disturbed the eerie silence. The senator fell back to the ground. He stared up at the trees above him, the leaves having begun to fall this year. His last on earth. The searing pain in his chest began to subside and his heartbeat slowed. Every stilted beat hurt, but not as much as the burning in his heart. In his last moment, he focused on one reddish leaf floating down toward him. He felt as though he was finally at peace. His wife and kids appeared before him. He hoped they were safe. He hoped his actions didn't put them in danger too. His watery gaze then clouded until there was nothing.

Jasiah Weston stopped his progress across the common area used for gatherings and celebrations. The animosity of the years gone by had lifted a few months ago, and they were actually living just as the other community members in Glen Hollow, the town at the bottom of his mountain. The truce had been made, the town had honored its promises to bring water and electricity up the mountain, and they'd begun to employ many of the people of Hickory Hills in Glen Hollow. The long-held argument over unpaid taxes had been satisfied and their former president, Craig Howard, was now dead and buried. And, peace had finally fallen over Hickory Hills.

The shot filled the air, the peace of a moment ago, now felt stifling and ugly once more. Feeling a twist in his stomach, Jasiah turned and moved deliberately in the direction of the shot. It was a sound that had gone silent up here. Except during hunting season, and that wasn't due for another month.

Jasiah entered the woods, his steps as silent as if on dirt. His years as a tracker had taught him well. He found his well-worn path through the trees, easily stepping over fallen trees and branches as he stealthily slid along the narrow passageway. A woman appeared from his right. He recognized her as one of the operatives that lived in the old sewing factory in Glen Hollow. They'd been instrumental in affecting the negotiations here.

Their eyes locked. He motioned for her to join him. The direction she was heading would alert whoever carried a gun they were near. She slowly inched her way toward him. He nodded, then continued his silent trek toward the shot.

Voices carried to them and he crouched to his left knee. The woman stopped behind him. He pointed through the trees to see a man, dressed in dark pants and a black hoodie standing before a man kneeling in front of him.

"I didn't know you were involved," the kneeling man said.

The woman behind him whispered. "It's the senator."

The hooded man's voice was emotionless when he replied. "You do now."

"Where's the recording?"

"It's with someone who making changes."

He pulled the trigger once more and the man with the white shirt, the senator, fell to the ground with a thud. The hooded man stared for a moment, then turned his head in their direction. Instinctively, Jasiah reached back to find the hand of the woman behind him. He squeezed her fingers, but his intent was to run like the wind if the man saw them. He didn't have his gun with him right now. The need to carry had subsided weeks ago.

The woman squeezed his fingers in silent reply and he held his breath. Turning his body, the man stared in their direction. The small copse of brush he and the woman had ducked behind would hopefully keep them hidden.

The hooded man stared for a few moments more, then turned and stepped over the dead man and moved toward the black road in the middle of the mountain.

The woman behind him stood, but he tugged her hand and pulled her back down.

"We have to stay hidden. I'm not armed," he whispered.

The smile that smoothed across her beautiful face mesmerized him. "I am."

She stood then and stepped on his path, following the man almost as silently as Jasiah would have done himself.

He spurred into action, following this brave warrior woman, as she stopped at the dead man's side, leaned down and placed her fingers to the side of his neck and waited a moment. She shook her head, her dark ponytail, swishing over her shoulders, then stood once again and followed the path the killer had taken.

Jasiah offered a silent prayer to the dead man and

pushed away the thoughts that this would bring bad things back to the mountain. They so needed to keep things peaceful up here. They'd learned as much after dealing with Craig these past years.

He caught up to the woman as quickly as he could, without making enough noise to wake the dead. Though he didn't mean that as a pun. Just as she reached the road, she knelt down and watched a vehicle careen down the road. She pulled her phone from her back pocket and typed something into it with such speed and efficiency it was impressive.

Since he'd only just gotten his first phone a few weeks ago, he felt at a total loss to this new skill he witnessed.

She stood and turned toward him, pocketing her phone in her back pocket as if she did it a hundred times each day.

"My name is Maya Sager." She held her hand out to him.

He took her hand in his. "Jasiah Weston."

"It's nice to finally meet you Jasiah. I'm sorry it's like this. Do you know who that man was? Was he one of your people?"

2

He was
She assumed he
massively and unrefined.

He had his hair cut short and a short beard. Basically, he was groomed, which was in contrast to her assumption of him.

His brows furrowed, then he shook his head. "No, he isn't one of my people. Are you assuming that because he killed that guy?"

"No, but he's up here on the mountain, so I wanted to make sure."

"So is that dead man but he isn't one of mine either. Is he one of yours?"

She sucked in a deep breath, eager to change the trajectory of this conversation. "Yes. Sort of."

She dropped her arms and tucked her thumbs into her front pockets. Footsteps behind Jasiah had him swirling around to face Myles, her brother.

Myles' eyes locked onto hers, the set of his mouth was

stern, his shoulders were stiff and slightly lifted. "Did you see the senator?" She asked.

"Yes." Myles then looked at Jasiah. "Who killed him?"

Maya took a step forward, so she stood next to Jasiah. "I don't know. We—"

she motioned between herself and Jasiah "—witnessed him being shot. The second time, not the first."

Myles nodded.

Maya motioned to the road. "He got in a car and sped down the mountain. I got the plate number and texted it to Tate."

"That's good. Maybe we'll still be able to get him."

"One of the others will have to do it. Tate asked that we stay here and guide the EMTs to the senator."

The sirens began to grow louder. She took another deep breath and turned to Jasiah. "You should tell your people everything's okay. They've likely heard the shots and they'll hear the sirens."

"How do you know he won't be back?"

"I don't. But he came to kill the senator, and he's done that. Unless he feels as though we saw him, which I don't think he does or he would have come looking for us, he'll be out of town by now, unless my team managed to get to him first."

"Why would you let him go?"

"I didn't let him go."

"You said you were armed."

"Should I have shot him down? In the back? Like a fucking coward?"

Jasiah's head jerked when she swore. She heard Myles chuckle, clearly entertained by Jasiah being affronted that a woman would swear. Or, whatever had caused his reaction.

"Of course not. But..."

Myles stepped toward them. "He was just a hired assassin. He'd likely not give us anything on who hired him, and we already know who hired him. We just have to get the proof."

The sirens grew louder and the crunch of gravel on the road signaled the ambulance was close. Jasiah turned as the ambulance stopped next to them, his shoulders were pulled back, his lips drew a straight line across his handsome face.

An EMT jumped from the passenger side and nodded at Jasiah. "Where's the victim?"

"He's back a few hundred feet. I can take you to him."

The EMT nodded and strutted to the back of the ambulance and swung open the back doors.

Maya touched his arm. "We can show them Jasiah. Please calm your residents so they aren't scared."

He turned his head and stared into her eyes. His were deep brown framed by thick lashes. The hair in his beard was dark, but not as dark as the hair on his head. There were even a few graying hairs at his temples.

"Thank you. I'll go tell them to stay out of the woods for a while."

He trudged up the mountain road, his stride purposeful and powerful. She watched him for a few steps, trying to remind herself she'd likely be leaving this town soon enough. After being here for two years and not having a single date, she was feeling a bit lonely and that's likely why he appealed to her. That was it for sure.

She turned to see Myles watching her. His brows furrowed, then his head turned to see Jasiah's retreating back.

The EMTs rounded the back of the ambulance, a gurney between them. She nodded. "Follow me."

She strutted past Myles, no words spoken, and headed

toward where the senator laid on the wet earth on the side of a mountain that had been the center of her attention for the past two years. Never did she think this would be the situation she'd be in all this time. A scared senator running for his life. The idiot running from the one place he'd have been safe, their HOG. Home, office, and garage. Where they'd offered him sanctuary. But, just as he'd done in life, he'd made another bad decision which cost him his life. Some people were their own worst enemies.

As she neared the senator's body, her heart felt heavy for this man who had ruined his life by getting involved in the wrong situation with the wrong people. The bigger issue now would be handling this moving forward. Did they let the world know the senator was dead? That would be a decision Tate would have to make.

The senator's white shirt stood out against the dark earth and the shade from the trees. She slowed her steps as they neared and moved off the path she'd followed to get them to this point. The EMTs set the gurney on the ground next to the senator. They followed their own protocol of checking for a pulse, opening a body bag they had strapped to the gurney and laying that out to prepare for a body.

One of them neared the senator's head, the other his feet. They bent and took hold of their respective ends of his body. "One. Two. Three."

The senator was lifted onto the gurney, his hands tucked to his sides, and the bag was zipped up, enclosing him inside. They strapped him down, then lifted the gurney. She and Myles each stepped to a side of the gurney and grabbed a handle. The senator was a large man, it wasn't an easy task carrying him over rugged terrain and stepping over branches.

Her dark long-sleeved shirt was damp under her arms as

they finally slid the gurney into the back of the ambulance. The first thing that came to mind was getting to the HOG and taking a shower. Then, hopefully she'd have some time to visit with Uncle Josh and Aunt Isi as they were here to congratulate Adelaide and Rafe on their engagement.

She sort of wished her own parents were here. Sometimes a girl just wanted a hug from her mama. Though she'd never tell anyone she needed a mama hug. She'd spent her entire life pretending she was tough as nails. She'd not ruin that reputation now. At least not to her teammates.

him to speak. Her hands wrung in front of her waist.

He smiled at her. "It's okay. Someone wandered up into [illegible] up here, but from Glen Hollow. The killer is gone. The special operatives down below are working on finding him. We're still at peace."

Elenor's chest heaved as she finally took a breath. The other women standing near her all sighed in relief and he realized just how each of them were still on tenterhooks worrying about their new lives and the gentle peace they finally found themselves in.

"Thank God," Elenor whispered.

Jasiah nodded, "We're still good. I don't like what happened, but it isn't anything we could have prevented."

One of the women, April, began crying and Elenor stepped toward her and wrapped her in a hug. "It's alright, honey."

April sniffed and swiped a handkerchief under her nose. "I saw a strange man hanging around here the past two days. I was afraid to say anything. He was big, and didn't look like he belonged here. He was taking food from some of the gardens."

Elenor patted her shoulder but turned her head to Jasiah.

"It's alright, April. You couldn't have known he'd be in trouble. I guess in the future, if anyone sees someone stealing food or lurking about as if they don't belong, come and tell me. I'll check it out."

April nodded her head and sniffed again. Jasiah nodded to her, hoping it would comfort her, but his focus was now on letting his father know what was going on.

He trudged to the home his father and mother shared, the heaviness in his chest growing with each step. He knocked softly, then turned the wooden handle and stepped inside, quiet as a ghost. His mom sat at the edge of the bed she shared with his father. She stood and hurried toward him as he neared the bed.

He whispered, "How is he?"

The crease between her brows told him it wasn't good news. "He's in and out."

Jasiah swallowed a hard knot in his throat and kissed his mother's forehead. He wrapped her in a hug and she whispered in his ear. "What's happening out there? I heard something like a gunshot."

He squeezed her once, then pulled back. "It was a gunshot. A townie wandered up here and brought trouble."

"Oh no. What will happen..."

He bent his knees and looked into his mother's worried eyes. "Hey. It's all good. The special operatives in town are on it. I was with one of them when the man was killed. She saw it all and knows no one up here is responsible. She's taking care of it."

His mom swallowed. Her eyes searched his. "Are you involved with her?"

His brows furrowed then lifted. "No. I didn't mean I was with her, with her. I meant she came into the woods just as I was making my way toward the shots. We were watching from a distance together as the man was shot the second time."

Her lips straightened into a thin line. "I'm sorry."

He moved around her and strode toward the bed at the back of the small cabin. His father's frail body lay on top with a sheet covering him. His breathing was shallow, his coloring a sickly gray. The gaunt features told of a man so close to death he had a foot in the grave already.

His dad hadn't been the same since he'd shot and killed the former president up here, Craig Howard. Craig was both his mother's brother and their entire community's menace. He ruled with an iron fist and there was no room for your own opinion. And he'd never talk peace with those who lived in town. Jasiah's father, Gerard Weston, saved a woman in town, who Craig was going to shoot. He was a hero. But the guilt he'd suffered since then, had taken its toll. He'd killed his own brother-in-law, his beloved wife's brother, and though just and right, it killed him inside.

Soon after that, he'd gotten sick, and even the doctors in town had said his illness was one that couldn't be healed, but his life could be prolonged and medication would make him more comfortable. Gerard had said no.

Jasiah perched his left butt cheek on the side of the bed

and picked his father's cold, boney hand up into his. "Dad. How are you?"

Gerard's eyes fluttered open. His lips spread open slightly, but he said nothing.

"Dad. Are you sure I can't get a doctor up here?"

His head moved side to side, then though his voice was weak, he said, "No. This is best. I've said my prayers."

"Dad, I'd love for you to stay with us."

Gerard looked into his eyes. Though Jasiah had the dark coloring of his mother, the pitch-black hair and brown eyes, his father's blue eyes always comforted him. Strong and firm instruction on all things of life. Hunting. Skinning a deer, rabbit, or squirrel came second nature to Jasiah because of his father's teachings.

"It's your time now, Jasiah. You need to lead our people. You need to keep the peace agreement and help our folks thrive. It's your time now."

Jasiah swallowed the hot rock in his throat and inhaled deeply. "I'll do it better with you here."

Gerard moved his head side to side and closed his eyes.

His mom laid her hand on his shoulder. "Even that little bit tired him out," she said softly.

Jasiah squeezed his father's hand then stood. He kissed his mom's temple and whispered, "I'll be back later."

He moved through the small cabin, his eyes landing on all the things his father had made in it. Cups carved of wood. Bowls carved too. Rope his father had woven from lambs' wool they'd collected from a farmer in town. Leather aprons for his mom made from the deer hides they'd tanned, hung on wooden hooks his father had made. This entire place was made from the love and skill his father had. It broke his heart that's all they'd have of him in a few short days. If he made it that long.

Sure, he'd have memories, but it wouldn't be the same. And, he'd truly be the man of the community up here, the heir apparent as they'd always done before him. The eldest son of the current president would then become president. Though in many ways it would be easy now, and not nearly as much responsibility because of the peace agreement. He wanted the Weston name to erase the Howard name in the history of this community, and he'd work his ass off making sure it did.

4

[illegible] pulled [illegible] the hook to her [illegible] in the towel, then pulled [illegible] towel from the hook and began drying her body.

What a shitty way to spend today. Seeing a man killed. She still saw how his eyes rounded when he looked at the man holding the gun. He knew him, that was a fact. They knew each other. The [illegible] in his actions. He'd hunted the senator through the woods, slowly as if he knew he'd catch up to him. That eerie calm that psychopaths had relishing the task at hand. He enjoyed his hunt. He took his time, mentally torturing the senator as he hunted. He also asked about a recording. She'd need to speak with Tate about that.

Slipping on her panties, and then her bra, socks, jeans, and a long-sleeved black t-shirt over her head, she pulled the towel from her hair and grabbed her blow dryer from the right drawer in her bathroom vanity. She flipped her head upside down, turned the blow dryer on and enjoyed the warmth coming from the end of it as she swirled it in circles, drying her hair.

Once her hair was dried, she tossed the blow dryer into the drawer, dragged a brush through her long hair, then pulled it up to the back of her head and wrapped a hair band around it, creating her signature ponytail.

With a heavy sigh, she opened the bathroom door and froze.

"What are you doing in my room?"

Her brother Myles sat on the sofa on the other side of her room. His right ankle rested on his left knee. His dark eyes stared into hers. "I wanted to make sure everything was okay."

"Of course it is. Why wouldn't it be?"

His right shoulder lifted in a half-shrug. "We don't watch people murdered every day. And, I noticed you were staring at Jasiah Weston a lot this afternoon."

She rested her hands on either hip and cocked her hips out to one side. "I'm aware this isn't a daily occurrence. I'm fine. I wasn't staring at Jasiah."

Myles sat forward and rested his elbows on his knees. "You were."

"What difference does it make?"

"Are you interested in him?"

"No."

"Are you sure? I haven't seen you look at anyone else like that since that stupid jerk in boot camp. What was his name? David or something. He was an asshole."

Maya chuckled. "He was an asshole. I really liked his give-a-shit attitude though."

Myles stood and tucked his fingers into his front pockets. "Until he didn't give a shit about you."

"Right. That's what makes him an asshole."

Myles chuckled. "Yeah."

She moved toward the door, to Myles' right. "Did you see Uncle Josh and Aunt Isi?"

"Not yet. I just got out of the shower and I think they're in Rafe's office talking things over."

Maya grinned. "Ahh, the big talk."

"Right."

Maya shrugged. "I'm going to find Tate and see if he needs a debrief. And, the killer mentioned a recording. He needs to know that."

"Why didn't you tell me up in the woods?"

"I didn't want the ambulance crew hearing it. We can't trust anyone."

"I'll go with you."

They stepped from her room and drifted toward Tate's office, across the living area from her room. His office door was slightly ajar, but she knocked on it anyway.

"Tate?"

"Come in."

She pushed the door open. Tate sat at his desk, behind two computer screens, his fingers flying over the keys of his keyboard as if he were playing a piano at a symphony.

"I'm glad you two are here. Let's debrief."

Tate stopped typing and faced them. Maya took the chair to the left, Myles to the right. They sat, almost simultaneously and Tate chuckled.

"Tell me exactly what you saw."

Maya relayed her information first. Every detail she could remember.

Tate listened to every word. He didn't type, he listened and stared at her. She knew what he was doing. Assessment was a big part of his job. He was making sure she wasn't negatively affected by witnessing the senator's murder.

"Do you need to speak to a doctor, Maya?"

"No."

"There's no shame in it."

"I don't believe there is. Look, it was a shitty thing to see. I'm sorry the senator was stupid enough to break out of here and get himself killed. I'm sorry it happened the way it happened. By the time I got to the point I could see him, there wasn't enough time to react and I didn't have a direct shot."

"Okay. I'm just making sure. You know this right?"

"Yes. I'm aware if I need to speak to someone, I can."

Tate grinned at her then shifted his attention to Myles. "Where were you while Maya and Jasiah were watching the senator's murder?"

"I came up through the woods from the side of the mountain. Since the caller said they'd seen someone walking around up there, I thought I'd see if I could find evidence that he'd been living up there."

"Did you find anything?"

"No. But, to be honest, we should go back up there and see if we can find the recording and any way he communicated. It may not give us much evidence, but it might. I know he didn't have a phone on him when he left here, but he may have found a cell phone or something, which can tell us how they found him here."

Tate nodded. "I wondered that myself." He took a deep breath. "Anything else?"

Myles shook his head. "No."

Tate took a deep breath. "So you two have visitors here this evening. I'm sure your aunt and uncle will want to see you. Tomorrow though, Maya I'd like you to go up and question the people up in Hickory Hills. See if they saw anything or heard anything. Maybe we can get some information from them. Make sure you see Jasiah first, we don't want to mess with the peace agreement. Myles, you can search the woods. Maybe a couple of the residents up in Hickory Hills will go with you. They know those woods better than we do. They may know of hiding spots and places to tuck into if someone would need to. Also, for the time being, we're keeping the senator's death under wraps."

"Sounds good."

Myles turned his head to her. "Ready to relax for a bit and have a drink?"

"Yes. Absolutely."

They stood, almost at the same time and Tate chuckled again. "You two are something."

Myles grinned then nodded toward the door. He opened it wide and waited for her to exit first. After he pulled the door closed, he whispered. "Maybe Mom and Dad are ready for a visit."

Maya looked up at her brother. They were twins, but he still managed to grow nearly nine inches more than her, which irritated the shit out of her.

"I think I'll call Mom and ask her," she mumbled.

As they crossed the living room to the kitchen, the door to Rafe's new office opened. Maya stopped and turned to see her Aunt Isabella exit first. She was as beautiful as ever. Her Hispanic heritage gave her all the good things a woman could want. Olive skin, dark eyes and hair, full lips, and though she was now in her late fifties, she was still stunning.

Maya changed her direction and moved straight into Aunt Isi's open arms. She felt the warmth surround her, and Aunt Isi's arms pulled her in tightly. She smelled great, as always. Whatever expensive perfume she wore, she wore it well. She and Aunt Isi were similar in height and build.

"Te amo sobrina hermosa."

"I love you too Aunt Isi. How was your journey?"

"It was fine. Josh is a good driver. Safe. He's always safe. So, we made it here in one piece." She giggled slightly.

"Uncle Josh would never forgive himself if he did anything to harm you."

Maya pulled away from her aunt and stepped aside to let Myles hug her. Uncle Josh stepped from the office just as she moved and he captured her in his big beefy arms and held her close.

"How are you little one? I can't wait to brag to your mama that I got to see you and she didn't."

"You tease her too much," Maya giggled.

"I do. But, she gives it right back."

Maya looked into her Uncle Josh's eyes and he winked at her as he stepped toward Myles. They hugged, a bit longer than usual, and Maya grinned. Myles needed to see Mama and Papa too. She'd call her mom as soon as she had a moment.

When Uncle Josh released Myles from his hug, he slid over to put an arm around Aunt Isi, as he usually did when she was near. Their love was inspiring.

Adelaide and Rafe stepped from the office next, Addy's cheeks were pink, so were the tips of Rafe's ears. The conversation in that office likely got pointed with Uncle Josh making sure Rafe understood what would happen to him if he hurt Addy.

Addy's eyes locked on hers and they held for a few moments. Maya raised her brows and tilted her head in silent invitation to have a chat, but Addy shook her head once then looked away. Maya would catch her later.

Uncle Josh looked toward Addy and nodded. "My little one is going to be a wife. I can't believe this day is here."

Addy's brows furrowed. "Thanks." Her shoulders

shrugged. "I'm not so long in the tooth that it was unlikely to ever happen."

Uncle Josh laughed. "I didn't mean that sweetheart. I meant, the time flew by far too fast for my liking."

Aunt Isi leaned toward Addy and took her left hand in hers. "Come, let's sit and have a nice chat with all of us. Jax and Dodge will want to know everything and we all know I'll be grilled until I spill every tiny detail."

Maya laughed. She was right about that. Her mama was fierce, determined, and loved her children with everything she had.

5

He would need to get a coffee maker, now that they had electricity and water up here. That was on his list of things to do. One of these days.

[...] common area from his. They enjoyed the sunsets on that side of the mountain. The thought made him simultaneously smile and feel awful. Inhaling a deep breath, he held it until his lungs burned. He hadn't been called during the night, so that meant his father was still alive, but for how long, was anyone's guess.

He stepped onto his parents' front porch and knocked softly with the knuckle of his forefinger. Without waiting for permission, he turned the handle and eased the door open. His mom stood at the newly installed kitchen sink as the water spilled from the faucet.

He grinned watching the wonder on her face. She turned to him. "I just can't get over this. Water comes right from this faucet. Just move this handle and water comes out. I don't know how many times I've done this."

"Yes. Amazing isn't it?"

She turned the faucet off and lifted the pan she'd filled to the stove. "Do you want some tea Jasiah?"

"If it isn't any trouble, mama."

"It's no trouble. I was hoping to get your father to drink some of it. Maybe we can get him to sit and drink."

"That sounds good. I'll go see if I can help him up."

When he moved past his mom, her hand grazed his arm and squeezed. His eyes focused on his father's prone form. He'd lost so much weight there was barely a wrinkle in the covers. The heaviness in his chest as he watched the shallow breathing threatened to consume him.

Sitting on the edge of the bed, he picked up his father's bony hand. "Morning, Dad."

He squeezed his father's hand gently, hoping to wake him, scared he wouldn't.

Taking in the thin hair on the top of his dad's head, which once had been a dark blonde or light brown, depending on how the sun shone on it. Now, it had lost all its color and fullness.

"Dad. Mama's making some tea for us to enjoy."

His dad's eyes fluttered opened. Their color had also faded, even more overnight. The light which signaled life, was fading away minute by minute.

The blank stare from his father made his heart twist. "Daddy." His voice cracked. He swallowed and sucked in some breaths. He closed his eyes for a moment and willed the moisture to dry. He needed to be strong for his mom. This would be harder on her than him. Though it was hard to imagine anyone would feel Gerard Weston's loss more than his son. They'd been inseparable most of Jasiah's life. Only during school hours were they apart. And, after he'd moved to his own cabin a few years ago, it was usually only in the evenings they were apart.

His father squeezed his hand and Jasiah opened his eyes and stared. "Dad. Can I help you sit up?"

His father moved his head side to side. "No," he whispered.

"You need to eat something."

"No." He struggled with a shaky breath. "I don't." He swallowed. "Not long now."

He lost the air from his lungs as if someone had just punched him square in the gut. He gave himself a moment to recover from the blow then he leaned in close to his father.

"You listen to me, Daddy. Killing Craig was the best thing you have ever done. He wasn't going to allow peace up here. Just look at Mama over there watching the wonder of fresh water coming right to her home. We have lights in here now and she's not straining to read her books at night. Or to sew or any other thing she wants to do. None of that would be possible if Craig were still in charge. His blind rage at losing control almost cost a woman in town her life. Thanks to you, she's still alive and I understand her and her husband rescue abused horses and bring them back to a normal life. That wouldn't be possible if it weren't for you. How in all that is holy can you just let yourself die because of one sorry son-of-a-bitch like Craig Howard?"

His mom hustled over to them. "Jasiah, don't yell at your father."

"I'm not yelling. I'm frustrated. He's a damned hero.

Instead, he's just lying here wallowing in some self-damned-pity because of Craig."

"Jasiah! You don't know everything."

"I don't care Mom. He may have been your brother, but he was insane with jealousy. He was out of his mind that he'd lose control. Daddy did us all a favor."

His mom's eyes watered and a single tear rolled slowly down her cheek.

He thrust himself off the side of the bed and paced to the kitchen. He turned at the door and saw his mom, lowering herself to sit near his father. His father's eyes met his across the room and he stared for a long time. Waiting for him to sit up. Acknowledge what he said in some way. Show some fucking emotion. Anything!

Nothing. Jasiah nodded ever so slightly to his dad as he reached back to turn the handle on the door. He pulled the door open, turned to step outside, the heaviness in his heart the largest burden he'd ever carried. Turning one last time toward his parents, he saw his father reach for his mother and she pulled him to a slightly sitting position. His father's eyes met his once more and this time he saw a tear trickle down his father's wrinkled cheek.

Feeling the same tear trickle down his cheek, he angrily swiped it away with his fingers, nodded once at his father and stepped out the door.

On the front porch, he sucked in a deep breath. The fall air was crisp this morning, the exhale swirled in a gray mist before him. Winter would be here soon.

Tires crunched on the road coming up the mountain and he turned toward the sound and cleared his head to tackle the next task - whoever was venturing up here today.

6

____

...as they secured jobs, they were buying vehicles and they needed a place to keep them, so a parking area was designated for this purpose.

...her from the center of the common area. She waved to him, then reached into her Jeep for two hot coffees from Lara's Delights. She smiled at Jasiah as she neared, a bit nervous about this meeting for some reason.

"Good morning," she called out.

He nodded and grinned, though it didn't reach his eyes. Her tummy felt the flight of a thousand butterflies, and she focused on not dropping the coffee. His demeanor was different than yesterday, and she wondered if he'd had a terrible night's sleep because of the senator's assassination.

As soon as she was close enough, she held out one of the

coffees. "Since it's early, I thought I'd bring you a coffee from Lara's. It's caramel and sea salt."

"Thank you." He grinned slightly and took the coffee from her hand. Their fingers touched and those danged butterflies took flight once more. She swallowed the enormous lump in her throat and occupied herself by taking a drink of her coffee.

He drank from his and his brows rose into his hair. After moving his cup, there was a bit of foam from the coffee on his mustache. She grinned and pointed to her lip. "A little coffee or cream on your mustache."

His tongue poked from his lips and swiped at the cream. "The coffee's good. Thank you. It's something I've recently learned about and had a couple of cups of. It's very welcome."

She cocked her head to the side. "What do you normally drink in the morning?"

He shrugged. "Tea. Usually. We make tea out of many things up here."

"I suppose you do. You'll have to get a coffee maker and make your own coffee. I don't know what I'd do without it in the morning. I need at least two cups to get me going."

Jasiah nodded. His eyes stared into hers and her heartbeat skipped. "I guess I do. Don't know if I'll ever be able to make it as good as this though."

"You can. Just buy the flavored coffee."

"Oh, is that how they do that?"

"Yeah." She shrugged, "Though, knowing Lara, she may have some super-secret recipe. That store of hers is popular and if folks could make it like this at home, she may not have the business she does."

She took another drink, scolded herself internally for acting like a teenager. She was thirty-four years old. She had more experience than most. She was a special operative for crying out loud. Talking to a handsome, smart, handsome, muscly, handsome man, shouldn't make her act like she couldn't carry a conversation.

"So, I'm up here this morning to see if any of the residents saw the senator around." Jasiah cocked his head, and she continued. "The man we saw murdered yesterday. Maybe someone spoke to him. Noticed him hiding or doing anything. We need to find out if he had a phone, there wasn't one on his body. We're trying to figure out how the killer knew he was here."

Jasiah nodded and took a deep breath. His impressive chest expanded and the plaid woolen shirt he wore couldn't hide his muscular build. "Yeah. A couple of the women saw him. Let's go see if we can speak to them.

She walked alongside him as they crossed the common area and headed to the south side of the mountain. It was pretty up here, and their cabins were nestled in where there was a flat spot. But, they were surrounded by trees and plants. Formal gardens were set up at the edge of the common area in neat rectangle patches. Chicken wire was wrapped around posts on the ends to keep the rabbits from eating everything they worked so hard to grow.

"Your gardens look lush."

His head turned to view the gardens. As fall approached, the pumpkins, gourds, squash, and other fall foods were plentiful.

"They do a good job up here for us. We have a few of the women dedicated to the gardens. They've kept us all fed up here for years."

She blanched a bit at the use of 'women' as in it was woman's work. But, she said nothing. It was likely that's just the way he'd always thought of it.

But she had to ask, "What do the men do?"

He halted and turned toward her. His lips curved up slightly, his eyes were clear and dark brown and very pretty. He'd likely hate hearing she thought his eyes were pretty, but they were.

"They hunt. Fish down below. They've built each of these homes. They chop the firewood that keep us all warm. They help till the gardens in the spring and basically anything else that needs to be done. We all just pitch in up here. But some of that work is back breaking. To be honest, I wouldn't care if a woman wanted to swing an axe to cut firewood, but it'd make me sad to see her have to work so hard when there is so much other work she could likely do."

Maya swallowed the lump that grew in her throat. She'd offended him and didn't mean to. Not really. She'd worked her entire life proving she could do anything her male counterparts could do. Addy did as well and actually so did her mom before her. But, being able to shoot a gun, learn to investigate criminals, learn skills that enabled her to do her job weren't nearly as physically hard as swinging an axe and lifting logs to build a home.

"Of course."

He nodded and continued walking toward a little home nestled between two large oak trees. It almost looked as though the cabin was built into the trees it was such a perfect fit. The door was darker wood than the rest of the home, one window looked out onto the common area. It was impossible to see the back of the home or see how big it was.

Jasiah knocked on the door and waited. The small stoop in front of the door wasn't large enough for both of them, so he stepped down and stood next to her.

A woman, who looked to be in her late forties, opened the door. Her eyes landed on Jasiah and rounded.

"Your father?"

"No, April. Not yet."

She let out a breath and whispered, "Thank goodness." Then her eyes landed on Maya.

Jasiah motioned to her. "April, this is Maya Sager from Glen Hollow. She's one of the special operatives living in the old sewing factory."

"Oh. Good morning." The woman was rather pretty. She had sparkling blue eyes and her light hair was pulled back behind a scarf on her head. Small blonde tendrils escaped the scarf.

Maya smiled at her, hoping she looked friendly. "Good morning, April."

"April, Maya is investigating the man who was killed up here yesterday. You mentioned you'd seen him around here. Can you tell Maya what you saw?"

April's eyes watered. "I'm so sorry he's dead. I hope he wasn't family to you."

Maya shook her head. "No. We were trying to help him. He snuck away from our home and ended up out here. We don't know how he got up here and what he did while he was up here. He'd been missing from our compound for three days."

thing
himself, and
He seemed hungry and
I just let him be. But if I'd said something,
maybe he'd be alive." Her eyes watered and Jasiah reached
for her hand.

"April, we've discussed this. You aren't responsible for his actions or decisions."

April nodded and pulled a handkerchief from her apron pocket and swiped at her nose.

Maya's voice softened and her smile was genuine. The little lines at the corners of her eyes were attractive. She was tough. He could tell that just by how she carried herself. She didn't seem afraid of much. She'd followed a man who she knew was a killer without hesitation. She walked with confidence, her back straight and her head held high. She was of Hispanic heritage, that showed in her coloring. He'd seen her a few times in town, and every time he'd seen her, her long dark hair was pulled into a ponytail on the top of her head. He wondered what she'd look like with her hair down, flowing around her shoulders.

"April. Would you like to sit near the fire?" Jasiah asked.

April's eyes snapped to hers. "Oh, lordy, I'm so sorry. Please come in, you must be chilly. These fall mornings are cool until the sun comes up high in the sky."

April pushed her door wide open and stepped into her cabin. Maya glanced at him, their eyes locked together for a moment. He nodded and held his hand out for her to proceed.

She stepped into April's cabin, and he admired the view for a split second. He filled his lungs with air and reminded himself of the job he had to do up here and that he'd need his focus.

"Can I offer you some tea?" April offered.

Maya held up her coffee cup with a smile on her face. "I have my coffee. Thank you, though."

April's eyes slid to his and he held his coffee cup up for her to see. "Maya brought a coffee for me as well. Thank you, April."

April motioned to the table near the fireplace. "Please sit down."

There were four chairs and he waited for Maya to choose her chair before selecting his. Maya sat quickly, not waiting for him to hold her chair for her. He hoped his mom didn't find out he wasn't a gentleman. She'd box his ears for certain. Even with her troubles with his dad right now, she expected he'd mind his manners.

April sat across the table from Maya. She folded her hands before her and seemed to be holding her breath.

Maya smiled again and sat forward. "April. When did you first see the senator?" Maya held her right hand up. "I'm sorry. The senator is the man who was murdered here yesterday. When did you first see him up here?"

"Oh, it was two days ago, I believe."

"Okay. And where did you see him?"

"He was near the garden. He seemed disheveled and hungry. He picked the green beans and ate them straight from the vine. He also ate a cob of corn without cooking it. He ate fast and he looked around a lot."

Maya nodded. "Why didn't he see you?”

"I was looking from my window." She pointed to the window that faced the common area. Her cheeks reddened. "I suppose I shouldn't have been spying on him."

Maya turned in her chair and looked at the window. She stood and moved toward the window and peered out. He enjoyed watching her. She was slender and small in size. Maybe five foot three or so. She wore black pants with pockets down the legs. She wore a black long-sleeved t-shirt, tucked into her pants. She had a holster in her waistband, concealing the weapon she carried. And, she wore a gun at her right ankle, based on the bulge in her pant leg.

Her eyes missed little, and he saw her envisioning what April had seen.

"So you looked out this window and saw him eating from the garden? Where was he standing?"

"He was on the outside, the far side. When he heard a noise, he'd drop to the ground and wait. I watched him for a while. Then, I locked my door and sat near the fireplace trying to decide what I should do."

Maya nodded. Her eyes met his. "I'd like to search the ground near the garden if you don't mind."

Jasiah stood. "I don't mind."

He turned to April. "Thank you, April. Do you mind if Maya asks you any other questions if she has them?"

Her bottom lip quivered slightly. "No. That's fine."

He offered April a smile. The poor woman lost her husband last year. Then the loss of Everett Howard, their president, Craig Howard's tirade and erratic and irrational behavior, then his death. Now, with his father's illness, many of the people up here were afraid of the next moves. April was a seamstress and made most of the clothes up here. A couple of years ago when Elena and her mom were still up here and making the elixir, they traded the elixir for fabric and sewing notions. It's all April had ever known as far as skills to keep food on the table. The peace treaty now left many wondering what would happen to them. April was one of those who seemed to fall between the cracks of the two societies. There wasn't much work in town for a seamstress. The old sewing factory the GHOST team lived in had been a large employer for years until they moved to the Lexington area. April now mended clothing for the residents up here, but there'd be a time when they didn't need those services and she'd have to find another way to survive. That would be his responsibility, to help his residents figure out what they could do for work.

Maya turned toward April. "Did you happen to see the senator anywhere else?"

"Only over by the first road. I thought he was leaving, so I ignored the fact he was here. I thought, maybe he was a townie who had fallen on hard times and was hungry. But his clothes didn't look like that, so I wasn't sure of his frame of mind or what I should do. His slacks looked as though they'd cost a fair amount."

Maya smiled and held her hand out to April. April stood and shook Maya's hand. "Thank you for your help, April. I'll do a little searching around where you saw the senator. Hopefully we'll find the information we're searching for."

April's cheeks turned bright red. "Oh, I hoped I could help."

"You did." Maya's smile was genuine. She was beautiful, that was a fact.

Maya turned to face him. "Do you mind if I head out to search?"

"Of course not."

She smiled at him and he felt the heat climb up his body like a fire licking his toes.

into her hairline. "Is that okay?"

He chuckled. "Yes. That's fine."

She let out a breath, grateful she hadn't done another [illegible] April had seen the senator in, she slowly stepped toward it. Her eyes scanned the area all around the garden. She circled the perimeter, a couple of times dropping to her hands and knees where the grass or vegetation was long to feel the ground for anything that might be there. She hoped a phone or some other communication device would be found. Tires on the road grew louder and she looked across the garden to see Myles' truck park next to her Jeep. She stood and swiped her hands on her thighs.

Moving toward Myles' truck, she noted Jasiah making

his way toward them as well. Myles stepped from his truck and moved toward her. "Anything?"

"Not yet. I'm searching the ground around the garden. One of the residents saw the senator stealing food. She said he'd drop to the ground when he heard something, so I'm hoping he dropped a cell or something."

Jasiah's footsteps stopped next to her. She turned her head toward him and saw him grinning at her. "What?" She tried ignoring those butterflies swirling around in her tummy. It was silly, really.

He shook his head. "Nothing. My coffee's kicking in I guess."

She laughed. "It'll do that for sure."

Pointing to Myles, she made introductions. "Jasiah Weston, this is my brother, Myles Sager. Myles, this is Jasiah Weston. You didn't meet formally yesterday."

She stared as the two men shook hands. They were similar in many ways. Myles' skin was a deeper olive color and Jasiah was definitely lighter skinned. But, both had dark hair and dark eyes. They were of similar build, though Jasiah stood maybe an inch taller than Myles. Jasiah was rugged. Creases around his eyes from years of working outside. His hands were calloused, and strong. Years of wielding an axe would do that. His shoulders were broad, his thighs looked solid. He was an outdoor man in all aspects. Her nipples pebbled thinking about all the ways he was rugged. She inhaled a deep breath and dropped her head to stare at the ground between their feet instead of where she wanted to look. Thinking about Jasiah like that would get her nowhere. They were from different worlds.

Myles started the conversation with Jasiah. "So, I'm instructed to comb the woods and look for anything the senator may have dropped. Can you spare a couple of men who know the woods to help me? We're happy to pay for the services."

Jasiah nodded his head. "I have a couple men here who know the woods better than they know the cabins up here. No payment is necessary. As long as our peace treaty is in place and everyone is abiding by the terms of it, we're happy to help you out."

"Thanks."

She glanced up to see Myles grinning. "You going back to crawling on the ground over there?"

"Yeah. After that I have to search along the road, and then I'll come and help you."

"Sounds good."

Jasiah nodded towards her, then turned to Myles. "Let me go get the men to help you. I'll meet you right here in about fifteen minutes."

He strode away and she had to fight herself not to watch him retreat. Myles grinned at her, she braced herself for a snide remark, but nothing came.

"Want some help while I'm waiting for Jasiah and his men?"

"Sure." She swiveled on her heels and headed in the direction of the garden. Walking around to the outside of it, she pointed to the ground. "I was searching here. April, the woman who lives in that house right there..." She lifted her arm and pointed to April's house. She saw April's face staring out the window at them. She smiled and waved and April disappeared. "Anyway, April said she saw the senator eating food from this garden and when he'd hear something he'd drop to the ground. I'm hoping to find something in the grass or in the garden itself."

"Okay."

Myles dropped to his knees and began searching just as

she'd been doing prior. They worked in unison for a few minutes when Jasiah and his men sauntered to the edge of the garden. Myles stood up, "Gotta go."

She waved as he joined them on the other side. She watched them shake hands and discuss what had to be done. Jasiah's eyes met hers more than once. A lot more. Which meant he likely noticed the same about her.

The heat crawled up her body and she blew out a breath which also blew her bangs away from her forehead. She heard his footsteps approach. They were steady and strong in their approach and her throat dried as he neared. He stopped and she glanced up at him.

"Do you need help?"

"If you don't have anything else to do. If you do have something to do, I can manage this. It's the easier of many things I'm usually doing."

"Like chasing after armed men?"

She sat back on her heels. "Sometimes." Laying her hands on her knees, she cocked her head to the side as she stared into his eyes. "Sometimes, it's stuff like this. Or, sneaking into buildings or computer research. It depends on the job."

His brows furrowed slightly as he continued to stare at her. His jaw softened and he looked thoughtful for a moment. "Do you like it? Your job, I mean? Do you like what you do?"

She smiled then. "I do. It's all I've ever wanted to do. Both of my parents have worked for GHOST. They're both semi-retired now. But, Myles and I grew up with our teammates. We played games like spy and covert ops. It's what I've always known I'd do when I grew up."

"And you get to work with your brother."

She chuckled. "And that's both a bonus and a pain sometimes. But, he'd likely tell you the same thing. It's just the two of us, and my parents love that we're able to watch each other's backs, just as they did for each other."

"I can imagine."

She studied his face a moment. The sun shone in the sky now, and when it landed on his hair she saw some gray at the temples. "What about you? Do you love your job, and do you have siblings?"

He swallowed and his brows furrowed briefly. "So, right now, I guess I'm between jobs. My father..." He swallowed again and turned his head to the right past April's cabin. "So, my father is on his deathbed. He's the president of our community up here. When he passes, it's been our tradition to pass the job on to the firstborn son. Not only am I first-born, I'm the only son, so then the president's job will pass to me."

"I'm sorry to hear about your father. He's probably a hero up here for freeing you from Craig's uncertainty. I know he's spoken of highly in town. He saved Everleigh from being killed. Our team, especially, is eternally grateful to him for that."

Jasiah's smile didn't reach his eyes. "He doesn't feel like the hero. He killed my mom's brother. He killed a man he'd spent much of his life with. No matter that Craig had become unpredictable and scary. He was family and my father has struggled with that since the moment he fired his gun."

Maya stood up and brushed her hands on her thighs. "I'm sorry that has weighed so heavily on him. I'm also sorry for your family's loss. I hope your mom is able to mourn properly and heal."

He smiled at her and it was so serene and beautiful she wanted to hug him. "She's focusing on my father, and that has preoccupied her for the time being. Soon, she'll have to grieve both of them."

Her nose stung and her eyes watered slightly. "I'm so sorry."

He inhaled deeply. "Thank you. She's strong. She has all of us up here to help her."

"So when you're president, what will that job entail?"

He tucked his fingers in his front pockets and looked into her eyes. "Right now, it means making sure the peace agreement is kept. It means ensuring we're doing our part to grow. By grow, I mean as a community. We have running water now. We have electricity and gas. We're getting used to that. I'm working with some of our builders and we're working on retrofitting homes with necessities. Just this morning I walked into my parents' cabin and saw my mom turning the faucet on and off in utter amazement. That might seem backwards to you, but it's a thing of wonder up here for so many."

She smiled at him and her heart swelled. "I don't think it's backwards. I think it's beautiful. How exciting to guide your people through such a new and exciting transformation. You should be so proud."

His grin was adorable. His cheeks pinked slightly and with the sun shining on him, he looked like something of a magazine figure. Real, but also, not real. How could a person be so beautiful he didn't look real?

"I'm proud. And, I'm learning all the new things I'll be responsible for. Just a few moments ago, it hit me I'd be the person to help April find employment. All she's ever done is sew. She makes most of the clothes up here. Once everyone is able to buy their own clothing, she'll find her finances in a pinch. I haven't the slightest idea how I'll be able to help her. But I'll figure it out."

Maya smiled. "We might be able to help you with that. Between all of us, we can speak to the folks up here and find out what they're good at. Didn't the mayor mention a job fair or something?"

Jasiah smiled and it was magnificent. "He did. I hate to admit this, but I don't see how a fair can help people get jobs."

She laughed. It came straight from deep in her belly. And, it felt good. "I never thought about that before. Actually, a job fair isn't like going to the county fair. It's where people who are looking for workers gather and talk to people looking for work. Hopefully, they'll all make a match and fulfill their needs."

His cheeks reddened and she saw him rub the back of his neck. "I guess I have a lot to learn." He mumbled.

She smiled softly. She'd embarrassed him and certainly didn't mean to. "I'm sorry for laughing. It wasn't at you. I actually didn't think of how a job fair would seem to someone who'd never heard of one. It is a silly name now that you point that out. And, to be honest, they aren't at all fun, like a county fair. But they can and do fulfill a need."

9

[illegible] some [illegible] with some girls [illegible] did his heart do a weird dance when [illegible] you around.

"I'm a bit out of my element. I have things to learn about how to blend some of our culture up here with your culture in town so we all merge easier. It's helpful that so many have gotten jobs in [illegible] us consider [illegible] a positive future."

"I have no doubt you will. It's clear you're a leader."

There it went again. His heartbeat did a somersault or something. Her smile was like the brightest sun. He pulled his shoulders back slightly at her praise. "I appreciate that."

He took a step back, "If you've got this, I do have to check on a few things."

Two men approached Jasiah. They nodded as they saw her, but turned to Jasiah. "You're being summoned to a council meeting."

"Who called a council meeting?"

"The inner council. With Gerard unable to fulfill his duties, we think you need to step in right now as president. This is not a time for us to not have a clear leader."

"Okay." He swallowed the knot in his throat, nodded to Maya, sad to leave her there. "Duty calls. I hope you find what you need. If you need access to anything else, please let me know."

There it was, her smile again. "Thank you. I'll let you know."

She dropped back to the ground, and he regretfully turned to follow his comrades to the building they also used as a church. It was nestled across the common area from the gardens, and sat out on a ledge, overlooking the eastern side of the mountain. During church services, the sun rose and he felt the love of God so purely it felt as though his soul split itself into several parts. God got his part, the mountain got its part, and there was some left to make Jasiah the man he was. And, was likely to become. This Sunday during services, he was going to pray about his heart feeling different when Maya was around. That was something new.

He stepped into the church and saw the inner council sitting in the first two pews. He strode to the front of the church and nodded as he faced them.

"Good morning."

"Good morning," was murmured back by all of them.

"Who wants to begin?" He grinned. He knew what they wanted, but he wanted to see who was stepping up as a possible vice president. Since he didn't have siblings and he didn't have cousins, and he didn't have a son, that position would step outside of the Weston family.

Reece Mansfield stood and nodded his head. "Morning, Jasiah. We were talking..." Reece motioned to the other men present. In all there were five of them.

"With Gerard's condition, we think it's important to have a strong leader. Craig's presence hasn't been completely erased and some of those who followed him are still running around up here. If they feel they can get away with things, they will."

"I agree with you, Reece." Jasiah looked toward the men. "All of you."

Reece exhaled. "We think you need to step up as president."

"My father is still alive. I don't think that's appropriate."

Cole Honeycutt, one of the men, stood. "How about interim president then?"

Jasiah grinned. "I can do interim president. I guess I've been doing that all along."

"We want to make it official tonight in the common area. Just have you stand up and say the council made a decision to have you named as acting president and you accepted."

He looked each man in the eye and saw them all waiting for him to say something. "I accept and agree."

A few loud breaths were expelled and Jasiah's heart constricted slightly. "Gentlemen, I get the feeling that there's still some lingering negative effects of Craig's leadership here. You all were worried about my reaction." He smoothed the back of his neck with his right hand. "I've never raised my voice, not once to any of you. Not in all my forty-two years. Why would you think that would change now?"

Cole swallowed. "It changed with Craig. He was certainly a much different man than you Jasiah. We all know that. He never let his feelings on anything go unknown. But, the second Everett Howard fell to the ground, Craig blasted his way into the president's position with more force than the dynamite he used on the base below. It's shaken us all a bit."

Jasiah stepped to Cole Honeycutt and wrapped a strong

arm around Cole's shoulders. He squeezed him and softly replied. "I am not Craig Howard. Yes, he was my uncle. But I am nothing like that man. I won't raise my voice. I won't hit, punch, or hurt any one of you all. Understand? That's not me. I am not that kind of man."

Cole's head bent toward the ground. "I'm sorry."

Jasiah's stomach twisted. "Nope. Not one of you has a thing to be sorry for. I see the effects we're suffering up here. I'll do my best to remove that horrible stain on our history. That's my promise to you."

Reece Mansfield stepped toward Jasiah with his right hand held out. "Thank you, Jasiah." He gripped Jasiah's hand firmly and held tight for a few moments. Jasiah's heart swelled with pride.

He reached forward and shook each man's hand and gave the same promise. "I'll do my best. I promise."

After they'd all shook hands, he strode down the aisle toward the door with a sense of pride. He couldn't wait to tell Maya what just happened.

He saw her the second the door opened. She sauntered across the common area toward the first road. She wore combat boots, and black slacks with pockets down each leg. He'd heard them called, tactical pants. She was petite in frame and size, but she was big in personality and warmth. She stopped crossing the clearing when she saw him. Turning toward him, they each neared the other with each new step. The light breeze blew her bangs around her face, her ponytail swished with each step. Her face, oh, he could stare at her face all day. She was a beauty beyond others.

"Did your meeting go well?" She slid her thumbs in her front pockets, and he chuckled.

"It did. They've asked me to step into the president's position as interim president so there's still a sense of leadership up here. In the event any of Craig's followers think they can create turmoil and distraction."

She smiled a bright, genuine smile. "I think that's a great decision. Your men must care for you very much." She turned her pretty head to and fro, checking out the area surrounding them. "After yesterday's event, I'll bet Craig's men are trying to figure out how to use that as an excuse. It's good you're in a leadership position to stop that."

He grinned at her. It came without thought. She was always thinking. "Yes, ma'am."

[illegible] the beginning

of informing my parents of the council's decision."

He took a step back, turned on his heel and headed toward a cabin to their left. She watched him stroll toward [illegible]. Also, sadness. What this meant, everyone likely knew, including his father.

The little cabin had a cute little porch on the front of it, two rocking chairs made of logs graced the porch. A small table to match nestled between them. It would be the perfect place to sit and enjoy a sunset or an evening.

Maya took a deep breath and swiped the answer icon on the face of her phone as it rang once again. "Hey, Tate, what's up?"

"Maya, I just received ID on the car you saw yesterday. It's a white Chevy Malibu. 2012. It came from a rental place in Brookswood. I need you to run to Brookswood and see what you can find out about the person who rented it when you're finished up in Hickory Hills."

"Okay. I won't be much longer. One of the residents saw the senator stealing food from the gardens and I've been checking them. So far nothing but a partially eaten cob of corn."

"Okay. He had to have something that let his whereabouts be known."

"I agree. Myles is in the woods with some of the men up here. I'm checking the side of the road where one of the residents saw him walking. Once I've done that, I'll head to Brookswood."

"Roger that."

Pocketing her phone, she glanced once at the cabin Jasiah had disappeared into, then turned and trekked to the edge of the road April had mentioned. She began by striding slowly along the edge of the road, then stopped in her tracks when a young girl stepped from the woods near her.

"Hi. You startled me." Her heart beat rapidly at the scare.

The girl grinned. She was missing a front tooth. Her light hair was pulled back by a headband made of matching material to her dress. Her black stockings had leaves stuck to them in places and she carried a heavy woolen jacket or shirt.

"I didn't mean to."

"No, I'm sure you didn't."

The little girl stared for a few moments. "You're pretty."

Maya smiled. "Thank you. So are you."

The little girl shrugged. "What's your name?"

"Maya. What's yours?"

"Marni."

"Marni's a cute name. Where do you live?" Maya knelt down to look Marni in the eye.

Blue eyes stared back at her. Maya wasn't sure if she was scared or trying to decide how much to tell her.

"I live next to the Westons. President Weston and Ms. Liliana."

"Oh, that's nice. I was just admiring their front porch. How old are you?"

Marni stared into her eyes for a few moments more. Maya smiled. "I'm thirty-four."

Marni's eyes widened. "Wow. That's kind of old."

Maya chuckled. "I suppose it seems that way to someone your age."

Marni shrugged. "I'm seven. My mama says I act older though. But I don't think she meant as old as you."

Maya shook her head and giggled. Out of the mouths of babes. "Probably not."

She glanced at Marni's stockings. "Were you playing in the woods? You've got leaves stuck to your tights."

Marni glanced down, swiped at her stockings a few times, knocking some of the debris from them. "Mama gets mad when I get dirty."

Maya laughed. "My mama never minded. She was usually dirty with me. My grandma, though. Oh, she always wanted me in dresses and frilly shoes."

Marni giggled. "You don't wear dresses now."

Maya's brows furrowed. "You mean today?"

"And yesterday."

"Yester..." Maya swallowed. "Did you see what happened in the woods yesterday?"

Marni took a step back. She pulled the woolen shirt she carried to her chest and wrapped her arms around it tightly.

Maya softened her voice. "It's okay, Marni. I'm just concerned you saw something bad."

A tear formed in the corner of her left eye and quickly slid down Marni's cheek. "I saw Senator Jackson get shot."

Maya scooted toward Marni. "Honey, I'm so sorry you had to see that. Where were you that you saw it?"

Marni swallowed. Slowly she turned her head and raised her hand toward the woods. "In there."

Maya lowered her voice. "Were you hiding?"

"No. I was in my playhouse."

Maya peered into the woods to see if she could see a playhouse. Nothing stuck out as a playhouse to her. "Will you show me your playhouse?"

Footsteps behind her on the road caused Maya to stand up and turn to see a woman striding toward them. Maya watched the woman's eyes graze over her, then to Marni, then back to her. Her demeanor was indiscernible, her shoulders were rounded, her midriff was full. She wore a dress without shape, her stockings were brown and slouching. When she spoke, it was as if she were tired and fed up.

"Marni. Where have you been? I've been calling you for lunch. We have work to do today. Daddy will be home from hunting soon, and we have to get the house in order."

"I'm sorry. I was in my playhouse."

Marni's mom stopped before Maya and huffed out a breath. "Who are you?"

"Hi. I'm Maya Sager. I live in Glen Hollow. We're up here investigating the..." She glanced at Marni. "The incident from yesterday."

Maya stepped forward to shake the tired lady's hand. The woman hesitated then gripped her hand and squeezed. Harder than necessary. It was puzzling.

"What are you doing with Marni?"

"She was telling me about her playhouse. I asked her to show me where it is. I'm searching for items the senator may have had in his possession."

"Marni doesn't have anything that belongs to anyone else. We don't have anything."

Footsteps landed on the road and Maya glanced around Marni's mom to see Jasiah striding toward them. His eyes took in everything. He was assessing the situation as he approached. She could see the emotions playing on his face, but she couldn't tell what he was thinking.

He stopped next to Marni's mom, but his eyes were locked on hers. "What's going on here?"

She gave Marni's mom a moment to answer, but she said nothing. In fact, her shoulders squared and her back seemed to grow rigid.

The silence grew uncomfortable, so Maya decided to answer. "I found Marni as I searched along the road. She just told me about her playhouse in the woods and I asked to see it. Then, her mom arrived and we've been chatting."

Marni and her mom said not a single word. It was weird. Jasiah turned his body to face Marni's mom. When she didn't look at him, he asked, "Is there a problem with Marni showing Maya her playhouse, Zara?"

"No." Zara never looked Jasiah in the eye. She didn't acknowledge him at all, other than to respond to his question.

Jasiah inhaled deeply. "Marni, can you show Maya your playhouse? Then I believe your mama needs you to go home."

Marni nodded. "Okay."

Zara turned and stalked up the road without another word. Maya looked into Jasiah's eyes. He offered nothing by way of explanation. "You okay then, Maya?"

"I am." She cocked her head to the right. "Are you?"

He huffed out a breath. "I am. Marni, don't forget to get back home right away when you've shown Maya your playhouse."

"I won't."

Jasiah nodded once then turned and followed Zara's path up the mountain road. Maya watched him for a while then turned to see Marni staring at her.

"He seems a little mad." Marni mumbled.

"I don't think so. He's different, but I don't think he's mad."

Marni shrugged. "My dad doesn't like him."

She turned and stepped into the woods and Maya followed close behind, so she didn't lose sight of Marni.

[illegible] forward, her back straight as she took a deep breath. After a few seconds, she slowly turned toward him.

"What do you need?"

"[illegible] Is there a problem?"

Zara's fists balled at her sides. "Should there be?"

Jasiah looked into her blue eyes. The whites of her eyes were red as if she hadn't been sleeping. Dark circles smudged her complexion under her eyes.

"Not at all. It's important we keep things peaceful with the folks from Glen Hollow."

Zara's words were short and clipped. "Does that mean we need to kiss their asses? It seemed as though you were doing a good enough job of that. Must we all?"

He flinched slightly at her raised and harsh tone. "I

didn't say you had to kiss her ass, or anyone else's. I simply said you weren't friendly with her, and I wondered what the problem was."

"I don't have a problem, Jasiah. I have work to do."

Zara turned abruptly and stalked toward her little cabin, next to his parents, where she'd lived since marrying Adam Jacobs.

"Jasiah?" His mom called from her door.

He hustled to her quickly, his heart dreading her next words. Stepping onto the porch, he inhaled a deep breath, and stepped through the door of the cabin.

Three things hit him as he entered.

The warmth. It was warm in here, the fire crackled and popped and the heat encircled him.

The steaming teacups sitting on the table. There were two of them. Both of them freshly topped off.

And, his father was sitting up in bed, and had a fresh shirt on. His father's eyes stared into his, and while he stared at his father, his image wavered as Jasiah's eyes filled with tears.

He sniffed lightly and swiped at his eyes, and he closed the distance between his parents and himself.

"Dad. You're sitting up!"

His father nodded.

"Are you feeling better?"

His father took a labored breath. The boney chest beneath the clean t-shirt lifted and fell with it. When he spoke, his voice was softer than usual, and a tad shaky. "You made me realize I've been feeling sorry for myself."

He swallowed a lump that formed in his throat. Not sure what to say, he sat at the edge of the bed before his knees gave out.

"I'm sorry if I made you feel bad. But, you were feeling

sorry for yourself. You taught me to handle things head-on, but you weren't doing that."

"No." He moved his head slightly, side to side, his voice slightly stronger.

"Are you willing to let the doctors from Glen Hollow help you?"

His father's faded eyes glanced at his mother before speaking, then to him. "I don't have the money."

"I'll get you the money. We'll make it work. They've offered assistance free. And, now that you're showing improvement, you can take back the president's position and the money that goes with it."

"No."

"Dad..."

"No." His father reached out a shaky, frail hand and laid it on top of Jasiah's hand. "I won't ever be strong enough again to be president. The doctors told me weeks ago that my condition could only be helped enough to give me more time."

Jasiah's brows furrowed. His heartbeat sped up so much it made him dizzy. "I have pancreatic cancer, Jasiah. That's why I refused treatment. I want your mother to have some means with which to live after I've gone."

"Why didn't you tell me this when you found out? You let me think it was you feeling sorry for yourself. You let me..."

His father's frail hand lifted as if it would stave off more argument. It did.

"Jasiah. Your mother and I spoke about it. There were things you needed to do on your own. One of them was coming to the realization that it was time for you to become president. And, the realization that my killing Craig was the only solution to what was happening up here. You confirmed that today. Both things."

His father's head swiveled to his mother, standing alongside the bed. "Lili, help me up."

Jasiah stood quickly, eager to help, but his father shook his head. "No. We've got this."

Liliana pulled the covers back to expose Gerard's skeleton-thin legs. He wore under shorts, but nothing else. His skin was the same as parchment paper. See-through and pale. She reached over and pulled his legs to hang over the side of the bed. His father's hand held his mother's shoulder for support the entire time. Jasiah sucked in a breath as he realized they'd been doing this for some time.

His mom, bent down, using her knees, her back was ramrod straight. She reached her arms around his father's body, clasping her fingers tightly together behind his father's back. His father's arms lifted and draped over his mother's shoulders and she softly counted. "One. Two. Three."

She straightened her knees as his father used all his strength to stand up.

His mom reached for a robe laying across a chair near the bed and quickly assisted his father in donning the robe. Once she'd tied the tie, she stood next to him, side by side, and wrapped her arm around his back as he wrapped his arm around her shoulders.

Step by achingly slow step, she helped his father to the table, nearest the fire. That's when Jasiah realized he'd seldom come here during the day. Always doing something outside. Hunting. Working on someone's cabin. Seeing to issues between the residents. Meetings in Glen Hollow for the peace agreement. This was his parents' routine and he didn't know about it.

His father sat with a groan. His mother moved one of the teacups to him and he wrapped his tired old hands around the cup as if to warm them. His mother moved her cup to the place next to his father then her eyes landed on his.

"Would you like a cup of tea Jasiah?"

His response was barely audible. "No." Clearing his throat, he tried again. "No. Thank you."

His mother sat and motioned to one of the two empty chairs at the table. "Please sit, Jasiah."

He swallowed again. All this emotion that welled up inside of him was over-whelming.

He gently pulled the chair from the table and carefully sat down, as if something would hurt him if he sat too quickly.

"Was that Zara I saw you speaking with?"

His eyes looked into his mother's for a while. "Yes."

All she said in return was, "Hmm."

Focusing his eyes on his father, he saw his father watching him. Lifting his teacup with two shaking hands, his father sipped at his tea, then slowly lowered the cup.

Finally he spoke again. "The most important job of my life was raising a good, smart, strong son. As the years wore on and Craig and Hanalore didn't have children, your mother and I talked about what that might mean for our family. Especially you. Then, all the changes began coming our way with the military installation being built at the base of the mountain and Craig's shear hatred and resistance to it. Then, when Elena left to live below and wasn't here to make the elixir, he had a few people try to recreate what she did, but it was never the same. Only that family, Elena's family, has the recipe. Craig grew more dangerous and unstable."

His father glanced at his mother, and she smiled the

softest, sweetest smile she'd ever given, and he continued. "That day I went down the mountain to find Craig, I knew if I found him, I'd have to kill him. To banish him would mean he'd be lurking around, causing trouble, for us and the townspeople. The sheriff couldn't guarantee he'd be put in jail, and that would only happen after he'd harmed someone."

His father took a deep breath. "When I saw him pointing the gun at that woman, Everleigh, I knew I'd be justified. But, Jasiah, I went down the mountain and didn't send anyone else, because I knew I was sick."

Jasiah's eyes opened wide. His mouth dropped open slightly as he stared into his father's eyes.

"I knew I wasn't going to be around long and anything they did to me, would be short-lived. It just so happened, it worked out the way it did for the good of all of us."

really like to be alive inside the forest.

"Do you like my playhouse?" Marni asked.

"I do. How did you find this?"

"..." in here and there was a small section of brush that had been pushed down, like someone slept there. I started stomping more of it down until it was big enough to play in here. Then, I brought some of my things here."

Marni reached into the dense brush on the east side and pulled out a woven basket. The long slivers of branches from this brush were used to make that basket and it blended perfectly.

"Did you make that?"

Marni's smile was wide. "I did. My grandma showed me how to do it. I make all sorts of baskets and bowls."

She reached in once more and pulled a couple of bowls, one had a lid tied with the weeds used to create the basket. "This is my favorite one."

She lifted the lid and showed Maya a collection of small bottles. They were empty, but nestled inside like little treasures.

"Where did you get the bottles?"

Marni's head bent down as she studied the ground. "From Elena's cooking room."

"Elena. Who used to make the elixir up here?"

"Yeah." She lifted a small bottle, it looked like a vanilla bottle. "This is my favorite one. It's brown."

Maya lifted the bottle and looked at it closely. It was definitely a vanilla bottle. She'd seen many of them over the years. The cooks she'd grown up with, and her grandmother always had real vanilla in the house, and it usually came in a glass bottle not plastic. "I can see why. It's pretty special. Do you know how Elena got it?"

Marni shrugged. "The boys used to go to town and dig in the garbage before the big trucks came to take the stuff away. They'd bring Elena little bottles and hope she'd fill it with elixir for them."

Maya set the vanilla bottle on the ground near Marni's basket and lifted another bottle out. An old cough syrup bottle. She grinned as she turned it in her hands.

She set that one down too. "Marni. You said the senator's name earlier. Did you meet him?"

Marni's cheeks turned a bright pink. She nodded her little head.

"It's okay. I'm trying to find the man who hurt him. If you know anything that can help me with that, I'd be so grateful."

"Would you get me more bottles?"

Maya chuckled. "Sure. I can get you bottles. All different kinds of them."

"Really? Even green ones. I saw green bottles once." Her smile was infectious.

"Sure. Green ones, and I saw some orange ones in a craft store once."

"Orange?" She giggled and clapped her hands together.

Maya looked into Marni's eyes. "Will you please tell me where you met the senator?"

Marni took a deep breath. "He was cold and hungry. I found him sleeping just over there."

Her little hand pointed to the brush, but toward the west of where they sat.

"Are you sure?"

"Yeah. I can take you there."

Maya grinned at this adorable little girl. "I'd love that."

Marni stood and pushed at the brush, then stepped through it. Maya stayed close behind her. They left the tallest brush and now navigated the woods as they'd done before. Some brush, downed leaves, trees, and large branches were lying about. It was evident Marni knew these woods like no other, the way she moved without needing directions, and stepped over debris like it'd always been right there.

Finally Marni stopped near a large rock jutting out of the mountain. It was three shallow walls of rock that created a small space for hiding.

"He was sleeping here." Marni looked up at her. "I saw him shiver. It was cold at night."

"You're very sweet. Did he wake up?"

Marni looked at the ground for a moment, then up at her. "I think I scared him."

Maya nodded her head. That made sense, he was on the run.

"Okay. Did you say anything to him?"

"I asked him if he was cold. He said yes, and hungry. He asked if I knew where he could find food."

Maya nodded but waited for Marni to tell her more.

"I told him about the garden. He thanked me. He asked if I had a cell phone."

Marni stopped and swallowed. She took a deep breath, her fingers began squeezing the woolen shirt she carried, but she said nothing else.

Maya squatted down so she was face to face with Marni. She smiled at the little girl, hoping to encourage her to keep talking. "I'm not going to be mad at you, Marni. You're helping me."

"My dad will be mad. My mom too."

"How about if I don't tell them? Your mom didn't seem to like me much anyway."

Marni squeezed her jacket again and nodded. "I brought him my dad's phone. Dad always forgets it because he's not used to using it and it's always laying in the kitchen. I brought it here for Senator Jackson. He was nice and he seemed sad and scared."

Maya reached forward and touched Marni's arm. She gave it a slight squeeze. "You're a very nice young lady."

Marni's eyes welled with tears and she nodded. "Now, I have a couple more questions."

Marni nodded.

"Did you take your dad's cell phone back home?"

"Yes."

"And, does your dad have it with him today?"

"No."

"Okay." Maya thought a moment. She didn't want to go

back on her word and tell Marni's parents, but she sure did need to see that cell phone.

Maya stood and heaved out a deep breath. She looked at the area where the senator had hidden, kicked at the grass around the area hoping to find the recording, then turned to Marni.

"So, I have a little bit of a problem. I don't want to tell your parents about the phone, but I do need to see the phone. Did the senator tell you about anything else?"

Marni's bottom lip quivered, but Maya kneeled down close to her again and hugged her. Marni let Maya hug her and reached her little arm out and hugged Maya back.

"Okay. So, let me ask you this. Can I tell Jasiah? Maybe he has a way to help."

"Will he tell my parents?"

"Not if I ask him to keep the secret first. What do you think of that?"

Marni waited for a while then her head slowly nodded. Maya's heart broke for this little girl. She'd seen a man murdered. Stolen her father's phone for him to use. And...

"Marni, did you tell your parents that you saw Senator Jackson get shot?"

Marni shook her little head.

13

Jasiah stared out at the mountains, the land his family had loved. His anger had been kept beneath the surface at not knowing about his father's diagnosis, and the fact they'd held that information from him never seemed to make it to the surface. Did it matter? Would it have changed anything? Only that he knew there wasn't anything doctors could do for his father, and the anger Jasiah felt about his father not seeking help.

But all the anger, everything that had taken place since the night Craig died, would have happened anyway. Maybe the timing would have been different, but the events would be the same.

He strode across the common area, his eyes landing on Maya's Jeep still parked where it had been all morning. He looked toward Zara's cabin, decided against knocking on her door. That wouldn't do any good for her or him. Adam Jacobs wasn't a man to test. Their past skirmishes had left them both aware the other wouldn't be taken down easily. But, an uneasy truce had been in place for years.

Inhaling a lung full of air, he turned toward the road and stomped down toward where he'd seen Marni and Maya talking earlier.

He focused on his breathing, slow and steady. He'd process this information tonight when he was alone.

He heard their footsteps on the floor of the woods before he saw them. Slowing his pace he waited until they appeared in the clearing near the edge of the woods. Several steps away from where he stood, they stepped onto the road. Maya smiled at him when she saw him.

He closed the distance between them. His eyes landed on Maya's hair. Leaves, dried brush and something that looked like a smashed berry hung from her hair.

He reached forward and pulled a couple of the offending fauna off her hair and dropped them to the ground. She chuckled. "The brush is thick in spots."

He grinned then looked at Marni. "Marni doesn't have stuff hanging from her hair."

Maya looked down at Marni and grinned. "Marni is smaller than me, and knows her way around the woods."

Marni grinned and his heart filled for her. Marni's life was less than it could be. He knew her father spent little time with her and her mother, well, that was an issue they'd spat about over and over.

Turning his gaze back to Maya he took in her eyes. The dark brown sparkled with life. Her skin was perfect. Smooth and clear. Her lips were full and he had an urge to touch them to see how soft they were.

Maya stared back at him and his heart thudded. Marni broke the trance he'd fallen into.

"You guys are gross. Mama said it isn't polite to stare."

Maya burst out laughing and he couldn't help it, he did

too. It felt good to laugh. Freeing. When was the last time he truly laughed? Was it sad he couldn't remember?

Maya nodded. "You're right Marni. It's not polite." She laid her hand on Marni's shoulder. "Is it alright if I speak to Jasiah about what we talked about?"

Marni's eyes moved to his. She pulled her bottom lip between her teeth and it appeared her eyes glistened with soon to be tears. Slowly, the sweet little girl nodded.

Maya kept her hand on Marni's shoulder. "Jasiah, we need your promise you won't say anything to anyone about what we're about to tell you."

Jasiah swallowed hard. His brows bunched and he rubbed the back of his head with his right hand.

"That seems to put me in a position. I need to know this won't harm anyone."

"It won't harm anyone. That I can promise you."

He sucked in a deep breath and let it out slowly. "Okay. You have my word."

Maya glanced once more at Marni, then looked into his eyes. "Marni saw the senator as he was shot. She also helped him get word to someone via a cell phone. I think that's likely how he was found up here. I need that cell phone so I can find the last number called and also run a diagnostics test on it for the tracking."

He cocked his head to the right. "What cell phone?"

Maya pulled Marni close to her and wrapped her arm around both of Marni's shoulders. "Her father's."

Jasiah closed his eyes. He took two deep breaths then opened them to see both Maya and Marni staring at him and waiting for his answer.

"That's not going to be easy Maya. There's bad blo...Adam Jacobs and I are not necessarily friendly."

"I know. He doesn't like you for some reason. But, I think I know how to make it seem innocent."

"How's that?"

"We'll need to visit each person who has a phone and ask to see the phones. We'll say there's a virus on the phones and I can help to remove it."

"How would you make them believe it?"

"I have a tracker unit in my Jeep. I can plug it into the phones and gather the information I need and it uploads to our server at the office. I'd like Adam Jacobs' phone first. But to make it seem legit, I'd go around to the other residents and do the same for their phones. We could actually have them all bring their phones to the common area later today."

"Are you sure you can make it seem like all the phones are infected?"

"I can make it seem as though we want to make sure they aren't infected. If we go to Marni's house right now, under guise of bringing her home and that I've just been informed of this issue, I can plug in to her phone and get what we need. Tonight, some of my team members can come with me and we'll rig up something to make it look legit."

"How did the senator get Adam's phone?"

Maya glanced down at Marni. Marni's sad eyes stared into his. "I wanted to help him. He said he needed a phone to make a call. He wanted to contact his family, and Dad always leaves his behind. He hates carrying it. So, I brought it to the senator and snuck it back home."

Jasiah knelt down and looked Marni in the eye. "Marni, honey...that was awful nice of you to want to help the senator, but I need to ask you not to do anything like that again. If anyone ever comes up here looking for help, I need you to promise me you'll come to me. Can you do that?"

Marni nodded slowly but said nothing. One lone tear slipped down her cheek and left a wet trail then dropped off her chin onto her dress.

Jasiah took her little hands in his and squeezed. "It's alright. I won't say anything to your parents. That's my promise to you. Okay?"

Marni nodded once more and Jasiah stood. He looked into Maya's eyes. "Okay. Let's get you what you need."

"It's called New Jersey Tea. The little flowers are what most of us use for tea."

[illegible] the tone light.

Jasiah chuckled in return. "No. None of those."

"What is that tree with the unusual white blooms?"

Jasiah chuckled. "That's witch hazel. We use that one quite a lot up here. It's medicinal, it's a cleaner, and it smells good."

Maya stopped and looked at the huge tree with the blooms that looked like mini fireworks. "I've never seen a witch hazel tree."

Jasiah and Marni waited for her to finish staring at the

tree in silence. After a few moments, she began walking once again and they continued on in silence.

She inhaled a few times as they passed by witch hazel trees and the fragrance was wonderful. Clean and fresh smelling. It never occurred to her to learn about trees and shrubs for their life-giving purposes.

They neared the edge of the clearing and Maya stepped forward. "Let me go to my Jeep and get my equipment. I'll be quick about it."

She moved ahead quickly, eager to get the information she needed. She'd upload that to Tate then she'd make the drive to Brookswood to learn what she could about the renter of the car she'd seen speeding away yesterday.

Opening the back passenger door, she reached into her duffle bag and pulled out the small hand-held monitor she'd need. It was smaller than her hand and zipped up in a case.

She grinned as she caught up to Jasiah and Marni. For her part, Marni seemed scared and apprehensive. Her face was taut, her eyes dull, and Maya's heart went out to her. It was quite possible adults had let her down before. She hoped they wouldn't do that.

Jasiah stopped in front of the door and knocked. The three of them stood side by side as the door opened and Zara appeared. Her eyes dropped onto Jasiah first. She stared for a few moments then her eyes swiveled over to her. Zara's seemed to harden for a moment. She squinted slightly then dragged her gaze away and landed her eyes on Marni.

"What's going on?" She nearly barked.

Marni softly said, "Maya needs to see something."

Maya spoke up then. "I've just been informed by my boss that some of the phones up here have possibly been infected with a virus."

"What does that mean? Phones can't get sick."

Maya shook her head quickly. "Not a virus like humans get. This is an electronic virus that can make your phone unusable." She held up her little monitor. "I can plug into the phone and check it for the virus. I've already checked Jasiah's phone and we'll be going around to check all the phones."

Zara hesitated for a moment, then disappeared. She came back a minute later with a phone in her hand. "He never takes it, and I don't know how to use it."

"I don't need to take it anywhere, I'll scan it here."

Maya quickly unzipped her carry case and pulled the monitor cord free. She gently took the phone from Zara and plugged it in before she could change her mind. Clicking on the monitor, she watched as the light turned green and the data transferred to it. There wasn't much data on it. Apparently Adam Jacobs hadn't embraced the cell phone lifestyle.

As soon as she got the green flashing light, she unplugged the phone and handed it back to Zara. "It's clean. No virus. Thank you for letting me check."

Neatly folding the cord into the case and zipping it, she looked at Jasiah. "Which one next?"

Jasiah nodded to Zara, "Thank you, Zara." He stepped back and turned toward the cabin he'd said his parents lived in.

Maya glanced at Marni. "Thank you for showing me your playhouse. I appreciate your help."

"You're welcome." Marni sullenly moved into the house and Zara stepped back and closed the door without another word.

Catching up to Jasiah, Maya fell into step with him. They trudged up the two steps to his parents' home and Jasiah stopped. "My dad is sick."

"I know."

"I don't want to worry them. But they have a phone and Zara would know that."

"Okay."

Jasiah nodded, then twisted the wooden knob on the door and pushed it open. He waited for her to enter, then stepped in behind her and closed the door.

The warmth inside the cabin was wonderful. She'd been outside in the chilly air all morning. Though she was dressed for it, she'd not realized how cozy it would feel inside.

A woman came from the back of the cabin. Her eyes landed on Jasiah.

"How is he?" Jasiah asked.

"The same."

Jasiah nodded. "Mom, this is Maya Sager. Maya, this is my mom, Liliana Weston."

Maya stepped forward and held her hand out to shake Liliana's hand. "It's nice to meet you, Liliana."

Liliana laid her hand in Maya's and squeezed gently. "It's nice to meet you as well, Maya. Jasiah has never brought a woman home to us before."

"Oh, no, I'm not..." Maya cheeks heated. "I'm only here because..." She couldn't give up Marni's secret. "I mean, I'm working with Jasiah."

Jasiah cleared his throat lightly. "Mom, Maya and I are working on the issue with the man who was shot here yesterday."

Liliana's hand flew to her face. "I'm so sorry."

Maya smiled. "It's alright. Please don't worry."

Jasiah chuckled. "We just needed to come inside for a moment, so Maya could warm up. We'll be heading out soon. She has other things to take care of today."

"Oh, well, it was nice to meet you, Maya." Liliana offered.

"It was nice meeting you as well." Maya turned toward Jasiah and waited for him to move. He leaned forward and hugged his mom. "Call me if he changes."

"I will, Son."

Jasiah, then placed his hand on Maya's shoulder and turned her toward the door. She liked the firm touch of his hand on her. When he leaned forward to open the door, she smelled his woodsy, pine scent. Pine and witch hazel. It was a fabulous combination.

[illegible] into her [illegible] they met. He looked [illegible] she was a bright spot in his day, and [illegible] something new. Prior to meeting her, each day was just another day. He was learning what he needed to do to be a good leader. He was an expert hunter. He helped build many of the cabins up here. Each day was just another day. But, yesterday, the murder aside, he'd met a woman he admired. She [illegible] unpredictable. That was exciting. It added to the excitement that she was a beautiful woman to boot.

He'd sat near the fire for the past hour, mulling something over in his mind. He'd felt the weight in his chest since his father told him he'd be president. He'd never really understood why that made his heart ache, but today it dawned on him.

He stood and brought his empty teacup to the newly constructed kitchen counter, complete with a sink made of stainless steel and a faucet so new it gleamed. He watched out the window above as the residents went about their day, he poured hot water from the kettle into his well-worn ceramic cup, dropped the tea infuser in the water, and waited patiently for it to steep. The next time he went to town, which would be tomorrow, he was going to look for one of those coffee makers. Maybe Maya would be willing to help him find one.

A knock on his door startled him to the present. "Come in," he called out. He cleared his throat and turned to see who'd knocked.

The door opened and Reece Mansfield stepped inside. "I got word you needed to speak to me."

"Reece, we need to ask all the residents with a cell phone to bring them to the meeting tonight. The GHOST operatives in Glen Hollow sent word there might be a virus in one or more of the phones and they want to help us out by checking them. They'll be up here in about two hours."

"Will do. We'll start spreading the word."

Reece bobbed his head, then turned. As he left the cabin Jasiah's shoulders slumped. He hated being in the middle of a lie like this. It went against all he believed in. But he also wanted to honor Maya's promise to Marni, and that little girl didn't need to be in trouble with her parents. They were tough on her as it was.

Turning, he grabbed the deer skin jacket his mom had made for him a few years ago for his birthday off the wooden hook he had made and stepped outside. Reece and a couple of others were going cabin to cabin spreading the word about the phones. Which would likely cause a bit of a ruckus. Because a phone virus was something they'd never heard of and that would likely scare them all.

He moved toward his parents' cabin. He needed his

father's blessing to do what he was about to do. He knocked softly, in case his father was sleeping and twisted the doorknob to enter. His mom stood before him, about to open the door. He smiled at her, "Hi."

"Hi."

Her brows furrowed and he glanced around her to see his father lying in bed, resting. The soft rise and fall of his chest confirmed life.

"I was about to come and find you. I understand there is a virus on the phones. I have your father's phone right here." She held her hand out with the phone.

"Thank you." He gently took the phone and slid it into his back pants pocket. "Is Dad too tired to speak with me? I would like his blessing before the council meeting."

She turned toward his father, whose eyes fluttered open. His mom nodded at him and Jasiah strolled to his father's bedside. Sitting on the edge he took his father's hands in his.

"The council is about to tell the residents that I'm to be interim president."

His dad nodded. "That's good."

Jasiah took a deep breath. "I'd like to tell them that soon that status will change. They will need to know eventually."

His mom neared and rested her hand on his right shoulder. Her silence unnerved him a bit then his father's eyes glanced at his mom, then back to him.

"Become president now, Jasiah."

"I don't want it like this."

"It's your duty."

"If we're going to be a new kind of community, we need to let the people vote."

His father's brows furrowed, and his head moved side to side. "It's not done that way."

Jasiah leaned forward slightly. "It hasn't been done in the

past, but I want it to be that way in the future. If we're going to successfully merge with the townspeople below, we need to begin acting as they do. They elect their own mayors and leadership. We need to do that up here too. I want your blessing to do this."

His father let out a shallow breath and closed his eyes. When he opened them, he stared into Jasiah's eyes for a long time. "I'm so very proud of you Jasiah. So proud."

Jasiah's eyes watered, and he squeezed his father's hands. "I'm the man I am, because of you."

His mother squeezed his shoulder. He leaned forward and hugged his father, then stood and hugged his mother to him. It was time to be the man he'd been taught to be.

Inhaling a deep breath, he stepped out of the cabin and strode to the center of the common area, where the residents began gathering. As was custom, he and the council stood at the front of the covered common area, benches arranged for tonight's meeting. The fire just outside of the covered area was already burning hot and would warm them as the sun set fully.

Smiles were bestowed upon him, as no doubt, everyone already knew what tonight's gathering was about. Tires on the road caused his heartbeat to ratchet up and anticipation of seeing Maya again filled him. He watched the road, and finally saw her Jeep drive toward the parking area and stop. Another vehicle followed her and parked next to her vehicle. Maya and Henry, whom he'd met at meetings in town, exited her Jeep. The other vehicle carried Myles and Spencer.

He moved toward them, eager to be near Maya once more, but also to discuss how they'd handle the phone situation with his residents. He smiled at her as she stepped forward, the urge to reach out and hug her was so strong it took his breath away. Myles reached forward and shook his hand, as did Henry, and Spencer.

Maya whispered to him. "They'll take the phones and plug them into our scanner, to remove any viruses found on them."

"Okay."

She smiled. "It's alright. We got what we needed. The rest is to cover Marni."

Pride filled his chest at the lengths she was going to protect Marni. That was a woman with a big heart.

"Thank you for helping her."

"Of course. I made her a promise and I'll do everything I can to keep it."

He nodded. "Okay. We're just about to start the meeting. I'll announce that they should give you the phones first, then we'll get to business."

"Sounds good. Where do you want us to be?"

Jasiah pointed to the table to the side of the meeting area. "If you'd like to sit at that second table, the residents will come to you."

"Sounds good."

Maya looked at her teammates and they nodded and began to sit at the second table.

Reece stepped up to him, "We're about ready to start, Jasiah."

"Thank you."

Reece turned to the gathering crowd. "Let's take a seat, we're about to start."

A bit of commotion ensued as folks sat at the tables, mostly in family groups. Children joined these meetings as well. Families greeted each other, small talk began to halt, and his community turned to face him.

Reece nodded to him and Jasiah stepped to the front and faced his community.

"Thank you all for coming. We'll begin with a prayer. Pastor Richards, will you do us the honor?"

Pastor Richards stood next to Jasiah and said a prayer. Jasiah bowed his head and folded his hands, his stomach twisted as the time neared for his announcement. It was right to do, it wasn't easy though.

'Amen' was said by everyone, and Jasiah inhaled a deep breath and his eyes landed on Maya.

"You'll notice we have some of the operatives from Glen Hollow joining us this evening. If you have a cell phone, they are here to check your phone for a virus they've been informed is circulating through the phones. This is not something that is contagious and though it sounds like a virus humans get, it isn't the same. They can remove any virus if one resides on your phone and this is mostly cautionary. So, please bring your phones to their table and they'll take care to scan it and remove any virus that might be present."

A few people moved to their table. There were maybe ten phones up here right now. Those who had gotten jobs had found it necessary to get phones for communication purposes. The idea of a cell phone had not been something everyone easily or readily embraced just yet. And the thought that these phones could contain a virus would likely stave off a rush at this point.

Reece stood once again, "We'll now install Jasiah Weston as our interim president." He turned to Jasiah, "Please raise your right hand."

Jasiah lifted his hand and faced Reece.

"Jasiah Weston, you are hereby bestowed the privilege and responsibility to act as president of our community. You agree to work for the people, to bring about positive change, and to help us integrate with the townspeople in Glen Hollow. You are given this privilege by virtue of your birth, and we honor that privilege and you."

Jasiah responded. "I accept this responsibility."

The people clapped their hands and Jasiah waited for the applause to end.

"Thank you for this privilege." His eyes wandered to Maya who bestowed the most beautiful smile on him. A tingle ran the length of his body.

He sucked in a deep breath. "I have the sad duty to share with you the condition of my father. The doctors have diagnosed him with pancreatic cancer. His diagnosis is terminal. There is nothing they can do to save him."

Gasps were heard, and some of the women cried. He waited for them to calm. Grateful for the moment to gather his own thoughts and emotions.

He lifted his hands to stave off the chatter. "I have another announcement. As we are now in a time of great change, I want our community to be as the townspeople below. Therefore, the office of president will be voted on. I am interim president and will act on our best behalf. But, in two weeks, we will have an election up here. I am announcing now, that I am a candidate for the president's office, but anyone else who may want to run, should tell a council member by tomorrow afternoon. Ballots will be drawn up and on Thanksgiving Day, a vote will be held up here for not only the position of president, but vice president, and the council."

The noise level rose and his eyes floated to Maya's. The soft smile on her face and the nod she gave him gave him strength. He nodded in return.

He then turned to Reece. "Will you please be responsible

for taking all names of those who want to run for office and keep them straight for the election?"

"Yes." Reece leaned in. "Are you sure of this Jasiah?"

"I'm sure. I want to be your president, but only if the people want me to be."

[illegible] she watched [illegible] what his people wanted. After all they've been through, this made him the best leader they've ever had in her eyes. Of course, she didn't know all of their history, but she'd never known a man like him before. The smile on her face was genuine and she couldn't stop beaming at him. As his eyes met hers over and over, she got chills at the unspoken message between them. Mutual admiration... [illegible] ...finally admit, she had a crush on Jasiah Weston.

As people filtered to the front of the meeting area to speak with Jasiah, she tried focusing on the task they were here to perform. Out of the corner of her eye she saw Marni and Zara, sitting at the back table, not moving. A man sat with them, his jaw clenched tightly, his arms crossed over his chest. Marni smiled softly at her, but in a way that hid her smile from both of her parents. Maya slightly nodded to acknowledge Marni but not get her in trouble.

Her teammates spoke to the folks who brought their phones up for scanning, reassured them there was nothing wrong with their phones, and were thanked for worrying about them.

Finally, Adam Jacobs stood and sauntered toward the table, zeroing in on Henry. He stopped at Henry's side and dropped his phone on the table. "I understand my phone was scanned earlier. I'm not sure why this phone was singled out by her." He pointed in her direction. "But, do you need to check it again?"

Henry twisted on the bench to look into Adam Jacobs' eyes. "Your phone was scanned first, because it was the first cabin Maya came to when she was alerted to the possibility of a virus on the phones. After scanning your phone, she felt it would take too long to go from house to house, and Jasiah told us of this meeting and felt that would be the most expedient way to get all the phones scanned. I'm happy to scan this phone again, but Maya is very good at her job and I'm sure she did a great job scanning it."

Adam Jacobs glanced at her, then snatched his phone from the table and turned on his heel. He barely reached the table where Zara and Marni waited for him, when he pointed across the common area to their home. Without word, they both stood and followed Adam home. Maya's tummy tightened as she watched Marni, head down, follow silently.

The crowd thinned around Jasiah and Maya stood to offer her congratulations. As she approached, his eyes bore into hers and the thrill that zinged through her body was both exciting and new. Excitement of being near him had her fingers shaking the closer she got.

"Congratulations, Jasiah. You are remarkable."

He shook his head. A sweet smile spread his lips. "It won't mean that much to me to be president just because I was born into the family I was born into. I want the people to want me to lead them and this is the first step in bringing our community closer in line to yours."

The fine lines around his eyes caught her attention and the fire's light danced on his face. Silver strands shone at his temples, and she noticed some silvery strands in his beard. He was mature, handsome, rugged, and strong. Not only physically strong but he was mentally and emotionally strong. She'd never met a man like him. He excited her.

"Impressive." It was the only thing she could think to say. He grinned and the beauty of the man smiling at her made her body do all sorts of funny things.

"Did you find out what you needed today?"

"Yes. Thank you. We did. We got the last number called and we've traced it to the person we believe was responsible. We're now adding that information to all we've collected to date. What my boss does with it from here is up to him."

"Good luck to you all for all you have to do."

She grinned. "So what happens for you now?"

He took a deep breath. Her eyes watched his massive chest expand and the tingles coursing through her body came back to life. "I will need to have a meeting with the mayor tomorrow as promised. I'll tell him what I've begun here. And we'll then begin planning for Thanksgiving up here. Do you celebrate Thanksgiving?"

"We do. We have a big meal and have a couple of drinks together. What do you do up here?"

"We all gather, share a meal, each family brings something to share and this year, as you've just heard, we'll have our first vote."

Her smile grew. "Progress."

"Yes. Progress."

They stood silent for a moment and he took in another

deep breath. "Would you like to have lunch with me tomorrow?"

Those tingles and butterflies twirled in her tummy. "I'd love that."

He nodded. "I'll pick you up at noon."

She swallowed. "I can't wait."

Reece joined them at that moment. "Jasiah, may I have a word?"

Jasiah nodded to her. "I'll see you tomorrow. I have things to take care of here."

"Go ahead, we'll be leaving soon as well."

When she turned to join her team, they were all staring and grinning at her. The heat that roared up her body nearly made her dizzy.

"What are you staring at?"

Myles stood and gathered the scanner he used. "We're watching you flirt with the president."

"I wasn't flirting."

Myles burst out laughing. "The hell you weren't."

Maya busied herself with packing up her scanner and notes. "It doesn't matter what you think it is. I find him impressive. Confident. And, smart."

"What about his looks? Do you think he's dreamy?" Myles stretched out the word and she felt her cheeks heat as hot as a cast iron skillet.

"I think he's very handsome."

Myles chuckled and sauntered toward his vehicle, Spencer close behind him.

17

Jasiah stood, looking out from his new kitchen and considered adding a bathroom to his cabin up here. The water was already brought into the house. He could surely add a shower and toilet. A couple of the residents up here had added showers and toilets to their cabins, and it was the talk of the town. The first day, there was a line outside of one house because everyone wanted the chance to see it work. It was pure joy watching his own grandmother when she saw the first toilet flush. That's only a small part of what he and his father had brought up here to the community of Hickory Hills.

He dressed, combed his hair and inhaled deeply as the excitement of seeing Maya again coursed through him. But, first, his meeting with the mayor. Snagging his deer skin jacket from the wooden hook near the door, Jasiah stepped into the fresh air he'd grown up with. He stopped a moment, turned toward the east, where he'd watched the sunrise an hour ago and he thought about his day. And, his life.

If his people didn't want him to be president, it would certainly hurt his feelings. He'd been good to each of these residents up here his entire life. He worked hard, just as hard as they did. But there were remnants of Craig still threaded into this community and only time would tell. There were still some who didn't like flushing toilets and vehicles sitting along the edge of Hickory Hills.

As he strode to his vehicle, the old pickup truck his father and he had worked on over the years, he waved to those outside working.

He stopped near the garden area, where three women were harvesting squash and pumpkins today.

"Good morning, Jasiah." Elsie waved.

"Good morning, Elsie, April, and Elenor. How are you this morning?"

Elsie responded first. "We're wonderful and so excited to be able to vote next week. Thank you for allowing this."

The genuine smile that parted his lips felt good. "It's really the only way. We all have a say in our lives now. It's freeing."

April nodded. "It is freeing. We've been excited all night."

"How do things look for our Thanksgiving feast up here?"

April stopped picking squash. She held up a beautiful butternut squash. "Plentiful. We'll have all the usuals. At last count, we'll have four squash dishes. The men have managed to hunt several turkeys. Elsie is baking loaves of bread. I'm making corn bread. And look at all those pumpkins. We'll have pies to go on for days!"

Her excitement made his heart fill with pride. "That's fantastic. I can't wait. I always eat far too much, but you're all such wonderful cooks, I just can't help myself."

"We need to keep you men fed. There's plenty of work for you to do."

He nodded. "That there is. I'm off to have a meeting with

the mayor. I'll be around later today if anyone needs anything."

Elenor stepped forward. "I'm so sorry about your father, Jasiah. I know I'm not a full-fledged doctor, but is there anything I can do?"

He placed his hand on Elenor's shoulder. "I'm not sure to be honest with you. But, you should absolutely ask that of my mother."

"I will. Thank you."

He smiled at the sad woman. "It's going to be just fine, Elenor. I know you're feeling a bit displaced right now, but you are part of our community and we won't let you starve or go without. That's my promise to you."

Her eyes glistened and he squeezed once again. He lowered his voice. "I have to go, but I mean it when I say you should ask my mother. She's been in solitude for weeks now with dad's illness. A friend, a cup of tea, and nice conversation is likely the best medicine for her right now."

"Yes. Thank you. I've been avoiding her because I wasn't sure what I should be doing."

"Do what you've always done, Elenor. Take care of us."

She straightened her spine and stood a bit taller and Jasiah's spirits lifted once more as he strode toward the old pickup.

As he started it up, he took in a deep breath and set his sights on his date today with Maya. His heart fluttered at the thought of having time alone to talk to her. He wanted to know all about who Maya Sager was.

He parked his truck in front of the two-story brick building that served as both the police station and the mayor's office. He walked into the building with a fresh sense of who he was. Today, he felt like he could conquer the entire world.

The receptionist stood as he neared her desk.

"Good morning."

He smiled. "Good morning. Jasiah Weston here to see Mayor Winters."

"Oh, sure. Let me ring him." She tapped the phone a couple of times. Her red fingernails glistened and he noticed her lipstick matched her nails. Her dark hair was pulled back with a red headband, which matched her red and white checked shirt. He grinned. "Rayleigh, Jasiah Weston is here to see you."

She hung up the phone. "He said you can go on in." She pointed a red fingernail at a door to his left.

"Thank you."

He stepped to the door, knocked once then twisted the handle and pushed the door open.

Mayor Rayleigh Winters sat behind a desk, a smattering of papers in front of him. There was a small stack of files to his right, and a larger stack to his left.

He chuckled and Jasiah looked into his eyes. "I see you're eyeing my work. To the left of me is the work I have to do today. To the right of me, is the work I've already completed. It's a bit lopsided, don't you think?"

Jasiah nodded. "Yes, sir. Looks like you still have a fair amount of work to do."

Mayor Winters stood and reached out a hand. Jasiah shook his hand then took a seat as the mayor waved toward the two in front of his desk. "Please sit down, Jasiah."

"Thank you."

Mayor Winters sat and crossed his hands in front of him on the desk. "How's your father?"

Jasiah took a deep breath. "I'm not sure if you've been made aware, but he is dying. Pancreatic cancer. I'm not sure he'll see Christmas this year."

Mayor Winter nodded once. "I'm very sorry to hear that and I had not been made aware."

Jasiah cleared his throat. "I promised to bring you updates as to our community and that's my purpose here today. Last night I was installed as the interim president due to my father's condition. But, I set in motion a change for our community. On Thanksgiving Day, our people will vote on who they'd like as their president. Anyone interested in running against me has until today to let the council know of their intent."

Mayor Winters whistled low. "Are you sure you want to do that?"

"I am. It's only right and it brings us closer to mirroring the community here in Glen Hollow. I figure with our residents coming down here to work, it's only a matter of time before they begin noticing some of the freedoms the citizens down here have that they don't. I'd like to set that right."

Mayor Winter sat forward. His stare was so long and intense it made Jasiah want to squirm. But, he didn't. He wouldn't. "That's very brave of you Jasiah."

Jasiah shrugged. "It's what's right."

Mayor Winters swept a hand through his graying hair. "What will you do if you are not elected?"

"I'll be looking for a job I suspect."

Mayor Winters nodded. "You let me know if that comes to pass, you hear?"

"Yes sir."

They chatted about trivial things and Jasiah's eyes swept over the clock above the mayor's head. Finally feeling as though the small talk was over, Jasiah stood. He had a date and he couldn't wait.

She laughed out loud. "You asked me to be your maid of honor when you were ten years old. Do you remember that?"

"...thought maybe you forgot."

Maya glanced at her cousin. "I didn't forget. You'll be my maid of honor if I ever get married, right?"

"Nope."

Maya's brows furrowed. "Nope? What in the hell does that mean?"

Addy laughed. "You should see your face." She turned in her seat so she faced Maya. "I'll be your matron of honor. Since I'll be married before you get married, I'll be an old married woman. That makes me a matron of honor."

Maya let out a breath. "Right." She shook her head. "I wasn't thinking."

Addy nudged her. "Speaking of, the guys said you were flirting with Jasiah Weston last night."

"I wasn't flirting." It came out a bit louder than she intended. "I was talking to him. I don't even know what they think flirting is. And, that makes me sad for their wives, because talking to someone isn't flirting. By that standard, I'm flirting with you right now. And, I don't flirt."

Addy giggled. "I've seen you flirt."

"The hell you have."

Addy held her hands up. "I have. Remember that asshole you were in boot camp with? David something. You flirted with him."

She shook her head. "I don't think I did."

Addy pushed her arm. "I'll take a picture the next time I see you flirt. But, until then, tell me about Jasiah."

Maya took a deep breath. "He's honest. Smart. Handsome. Caring. Do you know what he did last night? He told his people they could vote on whether he'd be their president or not. He could have just accepted the position handed to him by birth, but instead, he is giving his people the opportunity to vote. It's simply the most selfless thing I've ever seen happen. Especially with the shit show we're dealing with now with president-elect King. I mean the comparison is so polar opposite it should be in the dictionary. Plus..."

Addy chuckled. "I'll bet you were flirting with him."

Maya opened her mouth to say something, but the white Malibu they'd been looking for pulled out of Flynn's gas station. "There's the car," tripped from her lips instead.

Addy grabbed her phone and dialed. Maya stepped on

the gas to get closer to the car. She was one block behind the car when Addy started talking.

"Tate, Maya and I have eyes on the car. The car just turned off of Main Street, left on County Road. We're following."

Maya navigated the turn onto the county road, and kept her distance, without losing site of the vehicle. "I wonder why he's still in town?"

"Rafe thinks because we haven't notified anyone of the senator's death."

"That's sort of what I think. But, I also worry he knows Jasiah and I, or someone, saw him kill the senator. He turned in our direction like he heard us that day. But then took off. And, he's also looking for some recording."

The car left the city limits out on County Road and Maya followed at a distance. The Malibu then turned right, and moved slowly up one of the mountain roads that led to Hickory Hills.

Her heart hammered in her chest as they passed the road. "Addy, we can't follow him up there. It'll be too obvious. Call Tate and tell him we need operatives out here."

Addy called Tate and Maya turned her Jeep around in the road. As they passed the mountain road again, she slowed, but there was no sign of the car up the road. She mumbled, "He's gone far enough up that we can't see his car from down here."

Addy relayed the information and Maya pulled over to park in the parking lot of Lara's Delights. It was out of the way enough that it didn't look suspicious for them to be there, but she could see up the mountain road from where they sat. She parked so the front of her Jeep could easily pull out if the car came down the mountain.

She and Addy watched and waited. Addy then softly

said, "You know Elena used to meander around those woods all the time without notice. I wonder if any of her paths are still available."

"I doubt it. It's been a couple of years. The foliage in the woods is dense."

"How do you know?"

Maya glanced at her cousin briefly then back to the mountain road. "I was in there the past two days. And, Marni showed me her playhouse and where she first found the senator sleeping."

Maya sat back, her shoulders rigid. "I wonder if Marni saw this man too. I didn't ask her, Addy. What the hell is wrong with me? I should have asked her that question. That's a given right? Did you see anyone else?" She groaned. "I'm so stupid."

"Don't beat yourself up. It's not that big of a mistake. Sure, you could have asked, but you didn't. The next time you go up there, you can ask her."

"I wonder if he's staying up there? Hiding in the woods like the senator did."

"It's a possibility. Though why wouldn't he stay in a hotel?"

"There's only one here in town. Brookswood has a couple but I'll bet he wants to be here close to the action in case he needs to finish what he started. As in, he knows someone saw him, and he hasn't found the recording."

Addy groaned. "That could be. So, what's he doing, hanging around up there hoping to overhear someone talking about him? I mean if he'd have seen you, he'd know who to go after."

"Unless he somehow knew, but also thought he was outnumbered and would come back later."

Addy tucked her hair behind her ear. "I don't like that at all."

Maya mumbled. "I don't either."

Maya's phone rang. She tapped the button on her steering wheel. "Sager."

"Maya, it's Myles. Spencer, Henry, and I are up in Hickory Hills. Tate said you saw the Malibu come up here."

"Addy and I are watching the road now. He went up the last road on County Road. I drove past and can't see the car anymore. Not sure if he's in his car or skulking around the woods."

"We're on it."

"Okay. Do you need us to do something?"

"No. The people up here said Jasiah is in town meeting with the mayor. Did it look like the car came from the city building?"

"No. He pulled out of..." She stopped. "Wait. He pulled out of Flynn's Gas Station. That's right next door to the city building."

"Hmm. That could be coincidence, or he could be watching Jasiah."

"I'll go to the station and ask if he got gas or was sitting there."

"Roger."

The call ended and she pulled her Jeep from Lara's parking lot and turned right toward Main Street. She pulled into Flynn's station. A quick glance into the parking lot of the city building showed Jasiah's truck parked near the front door of the mayor's office entrance. Something similar to a hot rock sat in the pit of her stomach. Jasiah might be in trouble.

She left her vehicle and walked into Flynn's station. "Hi there, Maya. How are you today?" Pat Flynn asked.

"I'm doing well, Pat. I just saw a white Malibu leave the station. Did it gas up or was someone sitting here?"

Pat tipped his baseball cap back and scratched the top of his balding head. He settled the cap back on. "Both. He put some gas in, then sat here for a time. He seemed to be watching the city building and doing something on his phone."

"Okay. About how long do you think he sat here?"

"I'd say about ten minutes. He pulled away from the pumps."

Her heart felt heavy. "Thanks, Pat. I appreciate it."

"You have a good day, Maya."

He waved to Addy sitting in the Jeep then went back to working on the vehicle he had up on a hoist.

Maya glanced at Jasiah's truck, then climbed into her Jeep and told Addy what she'd found out.

Addy stared across the street at Jasiah's truck and the front entrance of the mayor's office.

"It's good that he isn't sitting here ready to shoot him. He left for a reason. What do you think that reason might be?"

"That's a great question." Maya started her Jeep, then turned out of the station and moved across to the city building. "I have a date with Jasiah for lunch today. So, I'll stay here and wait for Jasiah if you can take my Jeep back to the HOG."

"You didn't tell me you had a lunch date. Sneaky."

Maya grinned. "Cautiously optimistic."

Addy giggled. "Looks like you won't have to wait long."

Maya saw Jasiah step from the city building. He looked up as she drove toward him. He smiled and waved and butterflies took flight in her belly.

"He is handsome," Addy giggled.

Maya replied to Addy. "Yep."

Parking her Jeep next to his truck she hopped out and closed the distance between them.

"Addy and I were working and I saw your truck here. I asked her to drop me off so we can go to lunch from here. Unless you have something else to do after this."

His smile stretched his cheeks, and he couldn't have been more handsome.

The door to her Jeep closed and she saw Addy making her way toward them. Jasiah smiled at Addy and held his hand out. "I presume you're Adelaide. I'm Jasiah. Nice to meet you."

Addy chuckled. "I'm Addy. Nice to meet you too."

"Thank you for taking Maya's vehicle home for her."

Addy grinned at her. "It's no problem. I'm hoping to have lunch with Rafe soon, so I'd like to take off. Everything's ready for me to go then?"

Maya shoved her cousin in the arm. "Everything is fine. Thank you."

Addy grinned. "Take care, Jasiah. She's not easy."

Jasiah laughed and Maya stared at him.

Addy jumped into her Jeep and waved out the window as she backed from the parking space, then turned and left the parking lot.

Jasiah watched her drive away then turned his attention back to her. "Are you hungry?"

"I'm a little hungry. How about you?"

"I'm very hungry. I didn't eat breakfast this morning. I ran out of time before the meeting. So, tell me the best place to get a good burger."

"Homemade in the Hollow has excellent burgers."

"Let's do it."

He opened the passenger door for her and she hopped up into his truck. It smelled like him. witch hazel and pine and woods. Fresh and wholesome. Her nipples pebbled and she squirmed in her seat.

Jasiah hopped up into the truck and turned the key in the ignition. He backed from his parking spot then turned and drove from the parking area.

She chuckled. "You already know where it is?"

"Yeah. I had lunch there a couple of months ago with my dad. It was before he got so sick. But, I didn't have the burger I wanted to have. So, I'm going to rectify that today."

"Which burger is that?"

"Their Everything Burger."

"Ohh." Maya leaned back and held her tummy. "I can eat for about three days on that monster."

Jasiah laughed and she stared at his profile.

"Why are you staring?"

"I think you're handsome." It tumbled from her mouth before she even thought about it.

He turned his face to hers. She saw him swallow. "I think you're beautiful."

19

He sat across from her and watched her face for the emotions he knew she'd have there. She was filled with

I'm not used to being treated as a woman. And by that I mean, at work and home, I'm one of the guys. Addy too."

He nodded. "I suppose you are. I hadn't thought about that."

She chuckled and shrugged. "My mom always taught me to be that way. It pissed her off when the guys treated her like "the little woman". When she first met my dad, he held the door open for her and she told him to stop it. He told her his mom would box his ears if he wasn't a gentleman, no matter how tough the woman was. And, to be honest, I think that was something she liked in the beginning, but, she fell in love with him because he refused to be anyone other than who he was and so did she."

"Your parents sound like interesting people."

Her smile was magnetic. "They are. They're coming for a visit soon. I hope you'll meet them."

He nodded. "I'd love to."

The waitress came to take their order. He ordered the Everything Burger and Maya groaned. She ordered a bacon cheeseburger. She wasn't a salad eating, fake woman who was afraid to be who she was. After what he'd heard about her parents, he'd say she was just like them and that excited him.

He grinned as their drinks were placed before them. "So, tell me all about Maya Sager."

She chuckled. Her dark eyes sparkled. Little tendrils of hair escaped her ponytail and laid against her face. She had the hint of dimples when she smiled and faint creases around her eyes that spoke of someone who didn't exactly live an easy life.

"Ah, well. I mentioned my parents. Both are GHOST operatives. Before GHOST, my father was a police detective in Tennessee. He'd been married, had a son, who was then killed in a car accident when his wife drove drunk. It scarred him in many ways. They have a tree planted for Adam at the GHOST compound in Indiana. It's sweet. It's also planted next to a tree my mom and Uncle Josh planted for their brother, my Uncle Jake, who was a GHOST operative and killed in the line of duty."

"That sounds like a family who has suffered much loss."

Her right shoulder hiked up and dropped. "I suppose it does. But, it doesn't define us. We love hard, fight, work, believe in protecting those who can't do it for themselves, and in bringing criminals to justice. It's a family legacy I suppose."

"I'd say that's an impressive legacy."

She smiled at his praise. "Thank you."

"You're welcome. I'm not blowing sunshine, as they say. Besides all of that, what is it that makes Maya Sager, Maya Sager? What is it you want out of life? What is your favorite color? What kind of music do you listen to?"

She laughed and he couldn't look away. "What about Jasiah Weston? Who is he?"

"I believe I asked you first."

"You did. But, I also want to know about you."

He took a deep breath. "You know some of the history of my family. For most of my childhood, my grandfather was our leader. He liked our separation from the laws that bind all of you together. But, he wasn't vicious like my uncle, Craig. He kept us moving forward, healthy, thriving in many ways. But, staying to ourselves. We had school every day to learn all we could about many things. We were taught to take care of ourselves. And, we had the elixir to help us pay for what we needed. But, our numbers began to dwindle. People weren't having as many children. And, many of us didn't marry or have children at all. I think that was the beginning of Craig's breakdown. He became volatile. He was unreasonable and as Hanalore, his wife, couldn't produce an heir, he became more and more unpredictable."

She nodded her head, but her eyes never left his. "I remember Elena telling us some of this."

"For the record, Craig was my uncle, but I am nothing like him. My father was adamant that I be a good person. And, as it became clear that Craig wouldn't have an heir and the leadership would move to my father, then myself, Dad spoke to me often about doing what is right. Treating people with respect. Values. It was important to him, that I be a good person. And, I love my father very much, I want to make him proud, always."

"He must be so proud of you offering to let the people vote."

Jasiah shrugged slightly. "I hope so. I know he's worried."

"Are you worried?"

"I'm not. Not totally. I hope they want me to lead them, but if not, I'll find work and be just fine. Initially, I was raised to do that. It's only been the past few years, maybe since I've been around twenty-five that my dad began grooming me for leadership. Before that, I intended to hunt, fish, build cabins, and do what is needed to take care of my parents and my own family if I ever had one."

Maya cocked her head to the side and smiled sweetly. "Why didn't you get married and have a family like many others?"

He swallowed. "You know, I've asked myself that many times. I had..." He winced. "Women. Interested in that with me. But, I wasn't interested in them, not enough to build a life with them."

She toyed with her napkin then stared into his eyes. "Zara?"

He nodded. "Yes. I dated Zara for a bit."

"Is that why Adam doesn't like you?"

"Yes. Mostly." He took a drink and the waitress appeared with their food. The smell of the burger was amazing and his stomach growled. Maya chuckled and dumped ketchup on her plate next to her French fries. "He's also a staunch follower of Craig's."

"Because you dated Zara or because he liked things the way they were?"

Jasiah shook his head. "I'm not sure. Of course we don't

have conversations. When he and Zara married, it was soon after I'd broken up with her. She got pregnant right away and tried telling me the baby was mine. I knew it wasn't. I don't know what she and Adam discussed about the baby. I suspect she may have said she wasn't sure. He sure doesn't treat Marni very nicely. But, she's the spitting image of her father, and that man isn't me."

Maya took a bite of her burger and he couldn't stop watching her. In between bites, he said, "Favorite music?"

"Country and some rock. Yours?"

"Country all the way and some bluegrass." He took another bite and after swallowing it, asked, "Favorite color?"

"Purple. Maybe black. Not sure. How about you?"

He chuckled and dredged a fry through his ketchup. "Green. Favorite animal?"

She laughed. "German Shepard dogs. You?"

"Deer. They're sleek, quiet, and graceful."

Maya's phone chimed. "Sorry." She mumbled. Glancing at the readout, she looked out the nearest window, then her eyes locked on his.

"Jasiah, we're growing more and more concerned that the man who shot the senator is now following you."

"Why would he follow..." He stopped and stared at her. "Do you think he saw us?"

"I'm not sure, but Myles' text said he just drove through the parking lot and the car was parked at the back. The man was inside and took off as Myles walked toward him. They're chasing him now. I saw the car drive up the last mountain road just before I stopped at the city building today. We had operatives up in Hickory Hills so I didn't say anything."

"Okay. So, he's likely following me. He wouldn't know you were here."

"Unless he saw us somehow, but I believe he's focused

on you. I think you need to stay down here until we're able to stop him."

Jasiah shook his head. "I can't do that. I have to be up in Hickory Hills. If my people are in trouble with him skulking around, I need to be up there."

"No one else is in trouble, it's you he's focused on."

"You think."

"We're getting pretty damned sure now."

"Well, I appreciate that Maya, but I'm not staying down here."

[illegible] his place [illegible] which was [illegible] appreciate your concern. But, my parents are up there. My father is dying and my mom is alone. I can't leave them at a time like this. Plus, I've just set [illegible] ople at a time like this, when a killer is loose, it'll look like I'm the worst coward." He leaned forward. "Maya, honey, I am no coward."

She stared into his deep brown eyes. She could easily get lost in the depths of them. Of him. He was everything she'd ever want in a man. "But, you might bring..."

"No."

"Jasiah, please..."

"No. Maya, no."

She sat back in her chair and took a deep breath. "Would you let me stay with you? I can be there as protection."

His left eyebrow rose and a small grin formed on his lips. "You want to stay with me? In my cabin? I only have one bed."

Whoa. What. The. Hell. Just. Happened? Electrical currents ran through her entire body. Her nipples pebbled so hard she could cut glass with them. The look on his face, turned to one of a dare. He laid a dare at her feet.

"One is all we need."

"That so?" He leaned forward and lowered his voice. "I think you need to know something. I'm a man, who is extremely attracted to you. If you're sleeping in my bed, we likely won't be sleeping much."

"Is that a promise?"

Now, both of his eyebrows jutted into his hair. "You've got it, baby."

And now, just in a few short minutes, she was going to sleep with Jasiah Weston while also protecting him. That seemed like...words escaped her. It seemed like something of a cheesy romance movie. It seemed they'd have probably gotten there eventually the way they were flirting...Son of a bitch, she'd been flirting with Jasiah.

"You're speechless now?" He chuckled. "Are you thinking about changing your mind?" He teased.

She slowly shook her head. "Oh, I'm not at all changing my mind. You've been flirting with me all day. It's time you put your money, or your..." She nodded to below the table, "Where your mouth is."

He laughed out loud. He was quite possibly the most handsome man on the face of the earth.

"Don't you mean, where *your* mouth is?"

Her eyes flew open wide but she couldn't stop the smile that slid across her face. It felt like a grinch smile, slowly growing. "Deal." She said it softly and enjoyed watching the look in his eyes as he thought about what that just meant.

If his reaction was at all a measurement, she was pretty freaking good at flirting.

Jasiah waved the waitress down. "May we get our bill please?"

Maya giggled, proud of herself. She wiped her hands on her napkin. Then, decided to test her flirting skills a tad more. She licked her fingers, slowly, sucking the tips into her mouth before moving on to the next one. Jasiah looked like he was about to jump her from across the table right in front of everyone. He watched each of her fingers move in and out of her mouth. His pupils, though hard to see with the depth of brown in his eyes, grew. His jaw clenched. And, he squirmed in his chair.

He huffed, "Geezes."

She smiled and packed that little tidbit away for later. He liked that.

The waitress dropped their bill off. "You can pay up front. Do you need boxes to go?"

He replied, "No."

He stood, stepped around to her chair, and before pulling it out for her, he leaned close to her ear and said, "You'll pay for that."

She giggled. "God, I sure hope so."

He pulled her chair away from the table, took her hand and practically hauled her to the front desk. He laid money on top of the bill. "Give the rest to our waitress." Then continued out of the restaurant, her hand firmly locked in his.

She finally got her head in order as they reached the door and pulled back, stopping his progress.

"Scared?" He said as he turned to look into her eyes.

"Not of you. I want to make sure the killer isn't out there."

He closed his eyes briefly and she tapped out a text to Myles. She received a reply instantly.

"We're chasing him to Brookswood."

"It's all clear," she whispered.

He didn't wait. He tugged her hand and they hurried to his truck. He opened the passenger door but before she hopped inside, he grabbed her by the waist and pulled her tightly to him. His lips dropped onto her lips and he kissed the shit out of her. His lips molded expertly to hers. His tongue wasted no time sliding across her lips then sliding inside her mouth. As their bodies touched head to toe, she felt the firmness behind his zipper and it excited her completely. The wetness between her legs was instant.

His right hand held the back of her head as he continued to invade her mouth. He completely possessed her with just a kiss. All thought left her mind. She was a blank slate, all with one kiss from Jasiah Weston. No wonder Zara was completely besotted.

He lifted his head, his eyes bore into hers. "Still want to protect me?" His lips parted into a huge smile as he said it. Obviously he thought that was funny.

"Oh, you'll feel completely protected when I'm on top of you."

"Geezes." He mumbled. He helped her climb into his truck and hurried around the front of it. She watched him the entire way. His dark hair shone in the sun. His lips were puffy from kissing hers. And, if she could see his pants, she'd see an impressive bulge there.

21

That combined with the fact she was stunning and smart. She was everything he'd ever looked for.

after that kiss. Just a kiss and he was so hard he could hammer nails. Her gorgeous head turned to face him as he backed the truck out of its parking space, and his eyes landed on hers when he shifted to drive. He locked eyes with her for more than a few moments, then forced himself to look away so he could get them up the mountain.

"Is anyone going to wonder why I'm going to your cabin in the middle of the day?"

"I don't care."

His jaw ground together. He did care. But, not right at this moment.

She laughed and he looked her way to see the absolute light coming from her. She was radiant.

He took slow deep breaths, the ache in his groin failing to subside. He had fleeting thoughts about stopping along the woods and having her in the truck. But, she'd mentioned being on top of him and he wanted to see that in his cabin. He wanted to see her there, naked and fucking him.

He drove faster than he should have, but he did it anyway. He turned toward the first mountain road, closest to the base, which came up the mountain closest to his cabin. There would be people out and about today, but likely not much would be made about them coming up there. They knew she was an operative and was working with them on security. He just didn't know how to keep anyone from bothering them for a couple of hours.

He'd have to lock his door, and ignore anyone knocking.

Pulling into a parking spot at the end of the lot, he glanced at Maya. Her deep brown eyes had been watching him. "Ready?"

"Oh, I sure am." She breathily replied and his dick got hard all over again.

"I can't hold your hand."

"I don't need you to."

He nodded, feeling a bit deflated. She reached over and grabbed his hand. "I want to hold your hand. But, I understand."

He squeezed her fingers. Opened his door. And hurried around the truck like his pants were on fire. Which was a great analogy. He needed to pull these britches off and soon.

He opened her door and reached in for her hand to help her down. She smiled, then winked at him.

She flippin' winked at him. Goose bumps formed on his

arms and across his chest and his breathing turned to light panting. What the hell was she doing to him?

She let go of his hand and walked alongside him as they crossed the south side of the common area. His cabin was on the east side, so it wasn't a long walk. He opened his door and breathed a sigh of relief as he stepped in behind her and locked his door. Before he turned around he slid his deerskin jacket off and hung it on the wooden hook then turned to see Maya's top land on the chair at the table. She stood before him in her black tactical pants, a pretty pink bra and a gorgeous smile on her face.

As their eyes stared into each other's, she unbuttoned and unzipped her pants and he did the same. She stepped from her pants and he stepped from his. She shimmied down her pretty pink panties and he shucked his briefs. He quickly shed his t-shirt and stood before the most beautiful woman he'd ever seen. She was his Helen of Troy. He'd read that book and always wondered what she looked like. The woman who had started a war because of her beauty. This was her. She stood before him now and he knew he'd start a war for her.

He rasped. "Take the band from your hair."

She smiled, but reached up and pulled on the band. Her hair floated down and around her shoulders. He watched her run her fingers through her hair and how it softly touched her shoulders.

He scooped her body into his and carried her to his bed. Her skin felt like silk. She smelled like oranges and coffee. Her legs wrapped around his waist and the tip of his cock touched her entrance as he walked and he about lost it. He kissed her lips as her body held to his. He slid his hands to her ass, and slowly let her slide onto his cock. She moaned and so did he. Their kiss muffled the sounds but they were there.

He lay back on the bed, and she unwrapped her legs, but straddled him. She rose up enough to look into his eyes then she began moving on him. Her breasts moved with every slide of her body on his cock. Her warmth wrapped around him tightly again and again. His fingers dug into the flesh of her ass and helped her move. She moved faster, as her hips gyrated forward slightly then up and down.

"Maya. Damn."

She moved forward again, her eyes locked tightly on his and her body stiffened as her lips formed the most perfect 'o' he'd ever seen. Goose bumps formed on her arms as her orgasm rocked her and he lay still, mesmerized by this Helen before him. He pushed himself into her twice before his orgasm rocked him back. His head pushed into the bed, his eyes focused only on Maya.

She leaned down and kissed his lips softly, her tongue sliding over his in the softest, sweetest kiss he'd ever had in his life. Her lips nipped his a couple of times, then she nestled her nose into his neck, and laid her head on his shoulder.

"Damn girl," he huffed.

Her giggle vibrated through his chest and his arms wrapped around her tightly. He drifted into a sweet sleep.

22

realized what had woken her. She lay nestled against a naked and very handsome, Jasiah. His arm around her even now. His scent wrapped her in a sense of calm and happiness.

Sadly, she lifted herself up, pushed back the covers, wondering when they'd covered up. She stepped toward her pants, laying across one of the kitchen chairs. Fishing her phone from her pocket she saw a text from Myles.

"Call me."

She swallowed as the situation came back to her in clear

focus. There was a killer running around. She dressed as Jasiah sauntered into the kitchen.

"That's so sad," he husked.

"What's sad?" She chuckled.

"You covering up your gorgeous body."

She fastened her bra from the back, then moved toward him. He instantly leaned down and kissed her lips. They enjoyed their kisses for a few moments, then he stepped back and tugged his shirt from another chair.

Maya reread the text. "That's so sad." She offered.

"What's wrong?"

Her head turned toward him, a saucy grin on her face. "You covering up your gorgeous body."

He chuckled. "Sassy."

She shrugged, "Myles asked me to call him."

"Okay." He slipped on his briefs, then his jeans as she finished dressing. "You want some tea?"

She smiled. "I would. Thank you."

She watched a moment as he moved around his kitchen with ease. It was nice watching him. He took care of himself, and her, without help. Self-sufficient came to mind.

She sat at the table and tapped Myles' picture on her phone. It rang only once before he said, "Where are you?"

"It's nice to hear your voice too. I'm up in Hickory Hills."

"We lost him. He drove into Brookswood and disappeared."

"Shit. Do you think he's coming back here?"

"I'd be surprised if he didn't. We're teaming up and will be watching around the clock. One agent will be watching the roads. Spencer has been setting up cameras to watch the roads down here. He'll come up there in a bit to set up cameras around the common area, focusing on Jasiah's cabin. Until we believe someone else is his focus, we'll focus on him. Can you ask around and see if any of the residents have seen this man?"

"Yes, I was about to do that. I'll start with Marni. The little girl who saw the senator."

"Perfect. Spencer will be up there in about an hour."

"Okay." She took a deep breath. "I'll watch for him. Who is on duty tonight?"

"You and me."

"Okay. I'll come back with Spencer and get my Jeep and supplies."

"Why are you up there without your Jeep?"

"I had a date."

Jasiah turned and grinned at her as he poured hot water into her cup. He dropped a tea infuser into her cup then set the pot on the counter on a hot pad.

Myles said nothing for a long time. "Also, Casper called today and spoke to Rafe. He's got everything in motion now. The VP elect has now been sequestered for safety reasons. The information has been taken to Congress and a full-on investigation is underway. Casper said, King's men will likely get very violent right now and we're to be watching everything and everyone."

"Okay. That's why Malibu Man is still around. He has to silence any witnesses. And, he must know that someone saw him. And, whatever is on that recording is damning."

"That's what we're thinking." He huffed out a breath, "Maya..."

She didn't want to get into anything with him, so she said, "I'll see you later. We'll talk then."

She ended the call quickly and knew she'd likely have to play twenty questions with him later tonight. She didn't care. She liked being with Jasiah. Which made her wonder if he needed to be discreet during this election thing.

"Do I need to slip out the back door so no one knows I was here?"

Jasiah sat in the chair next to her. "Are you asking if I want to keep this a secret? If I'm embarrassed being with you?"

She shrugged a shoulder. "I suppose."

He laughed. "I'm not like that." His hand slid across the tabletop and closed over hers. "I like you, Maya. I'm absolutely enamored with you. I think you're stunning and smart and fun. I'm not ashamed to be with you."

"But, with the election, aren't you worried?"

"Look, from what I've heard and seen, your elections have gotten downright nasty. Awful even. We're not like that here. I hope we never are. I'm a grown man who is attracted to a grown woman. I'm single. You're single. We're consenting adults. I don't need to hide or prove anything other than I'm a good leader. I've been proving that my entire life."

Her shoulders relaxed. "Thank you. For the record, I'm absolutely attracted to you. You're amazing."

He laughed. "That's settled. So, I need to check on my father and I have other things I need to do. Do you need a ride down to get your vehicle?"

"No. Spencer is coming up here to install cameras. Also, we'll be watching the roads and up here around the clock to find the man who killed the senator and is likely tracking you. And, I need to speak with Marni."

"Okay. Do you need me to come with you to ask Zara if you can speak to Marni?"

"No. I'm a big girl."

"If she gives you any trouble, let me know."

He leaned in and kissed her lips and she kissed his right back. Man, he was something.

He pulled back slightly, "Will you be here later?"

"I have to work tonight. I'm not sure what my assignment will be yet. Can I let you know?"

"I feel safer when you're here!" His grin said it all. "You know, on top of me."

"I'm not telling my brother, or my boss that."

His laugh filled the room and her heart skipped a beat.

[illegible] next. [illegible] both for a [illegible] his head on his father's chest. It [illegible] and fell. He inhaled deeply, then turned quietly to let them rest.

"Jasiah," his mother whispered.

He waved, whispering. "Go ahead and rest, I'll come back later."

She sat slightly and [illegible] with it. She nodded in return then laid back down.

He softly stepped outside and crossed the common area to the covered gathering area. He sat at the front table, where he'd stood last night and soon saw Reece approaching.

"Good afternoon," he greeted.

"Afternoon. You only have one challenger. Adam Jacobs."

Jasiah sighed. "That's not surprising. What's his demeanor?"

Reece sat across from him at the table. "The same as always. Confrontational. Combative. Arrogant."

Jasiah nodded and took a deep breath. He'd been dealing with Adam Jacobs for eight years now in this fashion. Before he'd dated Zara, they didn't have any issues. But, Jasiah slept with Zara and she'd developed feelings for him and that was a mistake he'd paid for over and over again. Had he known that Adam had feelings for Zara, he'd never have dated her.

"Okay. And, what are his chances up here?"

Reece laughed. "I suppose you can't really discount him, 'cause he won't want to be embarrassed, but I don't think there are many up here who believe Craig's way was a good way. We have water up here now. We have electricity and gas. We're embracing it. People are getting jobs down below, and right now, if you want my opinion, the best thing you could do is help Max Couper and Elle Miller get permits to open their own businesses up here. Coup wants to open a woodworking shop. He'll sell wooden bowls, decorative plates, vases, and cutting boards made from wood. Elle wants to use her weaving and sewing skills to make baskets, trivets, hats, purses, bags and such. She saw them in a shop in Glen Hollow and wants to see if she can open her own shop with them."

"I'd heard some rumors to that effect. I can call the mayor and ask what I'd need to do to help them. That would also bring customers up here. Is that what they want? Do the residents want customers to start venturing up here?"

Reece grinned. "I have an idea. Let's get them together and ask that question. You call the mayor and I'll start spreading the word you want to have a..." Reece's brows furrowed.

Jasiah laughed. "I've heard them called fireside chats in town."

"Perfect. You'll have a fireside chat tomorrow night. We'll make it informal and sit around the fire."

"That sounds good."

Maya left his cabin and walked across the common area toward Zara's cabin. Jasiah couldn't stop watching her.

Reece whistled low. "I never thought I'd see it. A woman has finally captured your heart."

"Who said that?"

"The way you're looking at her says it. That's who."

Jasiah watched Maya knock on Zara's door. Zara opened it, stepped back when she saw Maya then glanced across the common area and locked eyes with him. Her mouth turned down in a frown, but Maya continued talking to her.

Finally, Marni stepped to the door and Maya spoke to her. They had a conversation and Zara crossed her arms over her chest, then ushered Marni inside. As soon as the door was closed, Maya stepped away and pulled her phone from her back pocket. Her fingers flew over the phone in that way he'd been impressed with when he first saw her. After she'd finished, tires crunched on the road and she stopped to see who was approaching.

Reece gently punched his arm. "See, captured your heart. Certainly your attention. But, man, you could do worse."

Jasiah watched Maya speak with Spencer, then begin unloading items from the back of his truck. She carried them toward his cabin and set them on the porch. She then approached him and Reece with a smile on her face.

"Spencer's here to install security cameras. He'd like to install three of them. One from the peak of your roof facing out. Which will also capture anyone approaching your door. One across the common area which will be in the tree. And one on this roof pointing out across the common area. That should capture everything except, your back door. So, I'd like to add one more to the back of your house."

Her smile was infectious. "Okay."

"Thank you." She nodded at Reece. "Nice to see you, Reece."

"Yes. Ma'am. Nice to see you too."

Her eyes then landed on his once more. He winked, and her smile grew. "We'll get to work."

She strutted across the common area and he watched her walk all the way across. When he turned his head to address Reece once more, he saw Zara staring out her window. When would she get over him? He'd promised her nothing. They'd actually only had sex a couple of times. There was no promise, no long-term relationship. Nothing.

"She gonna be an issue?" He quietly asked Reece.

"Zara or Maya?"

"Zara. Maya is mine. She's with me. If that bothers the people and they vote for Adam, then so be it."

Reece looked over his shoulder at Zara's cabin. "I don't think so. She doesn't have a happy life with Adam. She sees you and it reminds her all over again what she can't have. And, she sees how you look at Maya. You never looked at her that way. So, there's that."

Jasiah blew out a breath. "Okay."

"What are the cameras for?"

"They think someone is following me. It's for security."

Reece punched his shoulder gently. "I'll say this, if you're going to fall in love, do it with a security professional." Reece laughed at his own joke, then stood and walked away.

Jasiah, sat for a moment, watching Maya and Spencer work, then stood and turned to see Coup. He'd find out what help he needed. Then, he'd see Elle and finally, he'd call the mayor.

24

Nadia watched as Spencer settled down ... dozens of times ... It was mundane work to her, but this was important. Now that she had developed feelings for Jasiah, making sure he was safe was task number one.

Spencer climbed down the ladder and nodded. "All I need to do is set up everything in our system. Does Jasiah have a smart phone he wants me to set this up on? He'll be able to see this too, and—"

"I'll ask him. How much time do you need to set up his phone should he want that?"

"Give me twenty minutes."

"I'll go check."

She dusted her hands then swiped them on her thighs as she made her way across the common area toward Jasiah's cabin. She knocked on the door, but he didn't answer.

She turned to see Jasiah coming toward her. His physique was a marvel to behold. Tall, strong, powerful. He had confidence. It showed in the way he walked among the people here. He was totally at home here and loved it. The residents seemed to admire him as well. They waved, smiled, and greeted him as he walked. A group of men were hoisting a large log to sit atop a wall being added to a cabin, and without hesitation, Jasiah stopped and helped them lift it up. His shoulders stretched his shirt and she got a thrill remembering her arms around them as he slid her onto his cock earlier. She'd repeat that over and over again. Goose bumps formed on her arms and an electric current slid through her body thinking about it.

Jasiah finished helping the men with the log and turned toward her once more. His smile grew as he neared and she resisted running to him. Oh, she wanted to throw herself onto his body and feel his power once again.

"Are you finished with the cameras?"

"We are. Spencer only needs to connect them to the GHOST computer system. And, he asked if you wanted it on your phone?"

"What? The cameras?"

"Yes. He can install an app and you can see the cameras and what's going on right on your phone."

"No kidding." He grinned then shrugged his shoulders. "Sure, that will be interesting."

She held out her hand. "Then I need your phone, and about twenty minutes to set it up."

He pulled his phone from his back pocket and held it out, but paused. "Hang on. I just need to make one call to the mayor first."

She chuckled. "You do that. I need to check the woods where Marni saw the senator. She believes she saw someone else but she's not sure. And, I'm not sure that's the truth, but Zara wasn't interested in letting her speak any longer, so I'll do my own investigating."

"Alone?"

"I'm fine. I'll let Spencer know what I'm doing and if I feel threatened, I'll put on a comm unit."

His brows rose.

"It's an earpiece I can wear and others on the team can hear me. If I need help, they'll be there soon."

He stepped closer and pulled her close by her shoulders. He leaned down and kissed her lips softly.

"Please wear the comm unit."

She grinned. "Well, when you ask like that, how can I say no?"

He kissed her nose then her forehead and she inhaled his fabulous woodsy scent.

Stepping back, he whispered. "Find out what your schedule will be soon. I gotta make a call."

She giggled to herself. Then replied, "You know I'm more than a woman for you to slake your sex drive with."

He turned before stepping inside his cabin. "Oh, baby, I know that for a fact."

Gah! That hit in all her naughty places. She felt it through her entire body. And, she wanted him to call her *baby* again. She'd always thought it was cheesy, but when it came naturally like it just did from Jasiah...well, she wanted more of that too.

Taking a deep breath, she calmed herself as she strode across the common area toward Spencer's truck. He always had comm units and extra supplies. He stood at the back of his truck, a laptop open on his tailgate, and a smattering of supplies laying around him.

"Jasiah would like the app on his phone, he just needed to make a call."

"Okay."

"Do you have extra comm units back here?"

"Yeah. In that black toolbox up there." He pointed toward the back of the truck box.

She climbed up into the truck and squatted down as she located a comm unit and put everything neatly in place as Spencer had it. Opening the box, she turned the unit on, inserted the earpiece into her ear and jumped down to the ground. Spencer had continued to work on the cameras as she worked.

"I'm headed into the woods to see if I can figure out if Malibu Man is still hanging around."

Spencer glanced her way, "Did you need another kiss from lumberjack man first?"

The heat hit her cheeks, her chest, even her ears burned. "Shut up."

He laughed and she called Myles.

"Hey."

"I'm heading into the woods to see if I can find the place Malibu Man was hiding out. I have a comm unit on and want someone on the other end. Can you attach one please?"

"Sure. But maybe I should come up there. I'm not sure you should go in alone. Things are heating up. We just got word that the senator's house was torched."

"Oh, boy. They know he's dead, but they didn't find documents."

"Right. Which means, they may have Malibu Man on a mission to kill anyone associated."

"Jasiah isn't associated with any of this."

"But he was in the woods and saw the murder."

"So did I."

"Right. Malibu Man may have seen you or not. He may now know there was more than one person in the woods. He could have seen you in his rearview mirror when you got his license plate."

"That doesn't seem plausible. He hasn't so much as followed me. I've been in public for him to target if he wanted to. But, the senator said the video was with someone making changes."

Myles took a deep breath and let it out slowly. She recognized his fight for control of his emotions.

"Look, Maya, we're stepping into the deep end of the pool right now. We all need to stay safe and do things smartly. Let me come up there with you. We'll search the area you want to search. We've done a sweep of the woods already, but since you saw him drive up the last road, we should do it again. But, let's do it smart. And, Jasiah is one making changes."

Her shoulders dropped. "Okay." He was making changes. Actually, he was the only one making changes.

"Hang tight, I'll be up there in about fifteen minutes."

"Okay. I'm helping Spencer until then."

...coursing through him. Her head swiveled toward him as if she knew he was eager to speak with her. Her smile bloomed like the most beautiful flower and his

She took two steps toward him when something whizzed past him and hit the wall of a cabin behind him. Maya ran full speed toward him, Myles on her heels.

"Get down," she yelled.

He focused on her expression, fear in her eyes. Another projectile whizzed past him and hit the cabin behind him again. That's when it finally clicked what was happening. Maya jumped at him and knocked him over. He lay on his back, Maya on top of him.

"Are you hurt?" she asked.

"Well, I hit the ground kind of hard."

"You wouldn't get down."

"What the hell is happening?"

A gunshot sounded again. Maya's head twisted to stare into the woods behind her. He lifted his head to see Myles' weapon drawn, slowly stepping into the woods. Spencer was right behind him.

"What the hell?" He asked again.

Maya's eyes locked on his. "Someone tried to shoot you."

That's when she sat up and began feeling his chest, looking for holes or blood.

"Nothing. Oh my God, nothing. He didn't get you."

"No, but you're putting yourself at risk." He twisted so she was on the ground and he was on top of her.

People took cover and he could see them peering at him and Maya and watching Myles and Spencer. Unreal that this had come up here again.

"Did you see who it was?" He husked.

"No. Did you see anything?"

He shook his head. "I only saw you."

Her face softened and her eyes met his and held.

He began to get on his knees, "We have to get to cover."

"You do. I have to go help Myles and Spencer."

"Maya..."

"Jasiah, this is what I do. Please, get to cover. I'll be back as soon as I can."

Maya scrambled to her feet and ran toward the woods where Myles and Spencer had entered. He got to his feet and ran toward his cabin. He whipped open the door and stood inside, door open, watching the woods. After a few moments, no more shots were fired and he stepped out as others gathered near their cabins or cover but not in the open.

Soon Maya, Myles, and Spencer exited the woods. Maya

pointed in several directions, grabbed her phone from her pocket, and made a call.

Jasiah eased from his cabin and closed the distance between him and Maya. As he neared her he could hear she was on the phone with Tate.

She ended her call and stared at him for a few moments. "We're heading down the mountain to chase him."

"I'm coming with you."

"Jasiah..."

"Shut up. Get in my truck."

Her eyes shot a dagger or two but she hustled toward his truck. Myles and Spencer jumped in theirs. He jumped in his truck and Maya instructed, "Go down the last road. Myles will take the first road and Spencer the second road."

He nodded and sped off toward the last road. They'd named these roads over the years. The first road was nearest the military base at the bottom of the mountain. The middle road was in between the last road and the first road. The last road was the furthest away from town, and the final road to be built. They'd built it themselves and it had taken some time. But they wanted a way to come down the mountain without being in the vicinity of town. He maneuvered his truck around the three cabins on that side of the mountain, then turned down the last road. As they drove down, his eyes roamed back and forth.

"Did you see him leave?"

"We saw him run through the woods as if he'd been doing it awhile. Heard a car start and take off."

"Okay."

He made the first turn in the road without issue. He went as fast as he was comfortable, car chases being rather new to him.

After clearing the second corner he yelled, "There he is."

"Get closer." Maya demanded.

She tapped her ear. "We have eyes on him."

He couldn't hear the return conversation if there was one, but her eyes locked on the road before them and he did his best to navigate the curvy road as quickly as possible.

"There," she called out.

He followed the white car, began to gain on him then, as if in slow motion, he slowed the car, reached his arm out the driver's window and pointed a gun back in their direction.

Maya yelled, "Get down!"

He ducked his head and swerved to the right, out of shot of the driver. After a shot was fired and he was far away from their location, he stepped on the gas pedal and hit the white Malibu in the back. The car careened across the lanes of traffic, spun in the road and pointed in the opposite direction.

"Jasiah, turn around."

He did as he was told, she made a call on her cell phone. "Tate, Jasiah and I are chasing Malibu Man. He shot at us, now heading into town. Myles and Spencer are coming down First Road and Second Road. Not here yet."

She put her phone down and spoke to Myles and Spencer in her comm unit. "Tate has Henry and Addy meeting us in town."

She glanced briefly at him, then calmed her voice. "You're doing great. Just keep following him. We'll stay on him as much as we can. The others will all be close soon."

He nodded and continued to follow Malibu Man. "He's turning on Glenwood."

She told the operatives on comm units the direction Malibu Man was heading and he navigated the corner as easily as possible. His heartbeat couldn't have roared any more than it was. Sweat beaded on his forehead.

Maya sat forward. "He's going into the hospital. Oh my God. All the people there."

Jasiah gritted his teeth and turned into the hospital parking lot. "Stop here." Maya yelled.

He was barely to a stop and she jumped out of the truck and ran toward the hospital. He stopped his vehicle, turned the key off and jumped out to run after her.

He caught up to her at the entrance to the hospital. They ran in and saw Malibu Man turn a corner and run down the hall. He took a door to the stairs.

Maya stopped. "I'll bet he's heading to the basement to find the senator's body."

Jasiah nodded, "That's a good guess."

"Let's take the back stairs."

They turned and ran down the hall in the opposite direction. Few people were around, a few nurses began yelling as they ran in the halls.

They whipped open the door to the stairs and hustled down the steps as fast as their feet would take them. At the basement door, Maya held her hand up and whispered. "Don't say anything."

She pulled a gun from her waistband, and eased the door open. She listened for movement but motioned for him to follow her.

They moved down a hallway, dimly lit by bulbs in fixtures and yellow lines of reflective paint running both sides of the hall. Maya pointed above her, to a sign that read, Morgue.

She turned the knob on the door and slipped in, nodding for him to follow. A man sitting at a desk jumped when she rounded the corner. "What are..."

"Shh." She held up her hand and whispered to the man. "Has anyone else come in here?"

He shook his head vigorously. Maya whispered, "Go to safety. Now."

He hesitated a moment and Jasiah felt sorry for him. With his thumb, Jasiah motioned toward the door and the man moved on shaky legs to the door.

Maya took a deep breath and stepped into a cold room behind the man's desk. Rows of square doors lined three walls. Maya glanced back at him. "The senator is in here somewhere and I'll bet this is where Malibu Man is coming in case there's something on him."

"Something like what?" He whispered.

"A zip drive, thumb drive, or other code or location where the files might be. He told his killer the recording was with someone making changes. That's you. Or, that's him."

He wasn't sure what a zip drive or thumb drive was, but codes and files, he knew about.

Maya moved to an alcove behind the door and motioned for him to follow her. They could see the outer office via the window from this location. The light changed and he saw the black hoodie Malibu Man had been wearing.

He motioned to Maya and she nodded. Jasiah mouthed "Gun" and Maya nodded again. Slowly she reached down and pulled a second gun from her ankle holster and handed it to him. "Shoot only if necessary," she whispered.

He nodded and held the pistol down for safety. The door opened slowly and his body tensed. They were met with only silence for a few moments, then he moved into the room and began opening and closing the square doors on the wall nearest the door.

They stepped from the alcove as Malibu Man frantically opened locker after locker. He turned quickly when he saw them and raised his gun. His shots were erratic and Jasiah pulled the trigger. The man slid down the wall of lockers and sat on the ground. A small red dot near his heart was the only sign anything was wrong with him. Maya trained her gun on him, stepped closer and kicked his gun away from him.

"What's your name?"

"Fuck you," he mumbled.

"I get that a lot."

The blue eyes that stared back at them began to fade.

Maya tried once again. "What was King's plan as to the senator? He couldn't find the recording, so what did he think would happen?"

Malibu Man shook his head side to side. "He wanted the world to know the senator was dead. No one to give evidence."

"We have the evidence and a recording of the senator verifying it."

Malibu Man shook his head slowly. "He wants everyone dead."

"How did you know the senator?"

All he did was shake his head. His eyes closed halfway and his head stopped shaking. His hands relaxed and his shoulders slumped forward.

____

[illegible] then took [illegible] spoke to her

"We're in the morgue. Malibu Man is dead."

Myles responded first. "Are you alright?"

"We're fine. We'll stand by until you get here. Call Tate. He'll need to speak to the sheriff."

She pulled Jasiah's hand for them to step back. Once they'd [illegible], he turned and wrapped her in his arms. She wrapped her arms around his waist and absorbed his heat, his scent, his strength.

His big hands smoothed down her back. She listened to his heartbeat settle to a normal rhythm and closed her eyes. As footsteps began to grow closer, she lifted her head and stared into his soulful eyes.

"Are you alright, Jasiah?"

"I'm fine. Are you alright?"

"I'm perfect."

He nodded his head. "I agree."

Her heart grew once more. It seemed to grow every time Jasiah was near.

Myles entered the room first. He stared at them in their embrace, then turned his head to see Malibu Man slumped against the wall of crypts, one of them slightly ajar.

Spencer joined them a few moments later and finally Henry and Addy entered the room.

Addy grinned at her, nodded to Jasiah, then stared at Malibu Man.

Henry turned to them. "You two alright?"

Jasiah responded first. "Yes. We're fine. I shot him with Maya's gun."

Jasiah handed the gun to Henry. "I assume the sheriff will need to speak with me."

Myles shook his head. "Tate will decide what happens next. He's on the phone right now with the sheriff."

Maya stepped away from Jasiah and addressed her teammates. "He didn't say much. He said King wanted everyone dead. No one to give evidence against him. He wanted the world to know the senator was dead, hoping that would stop the wheels of justice from moving forward."

Addy took Malibu Man's picture, removed his hood and took another one. Jasiah's expression was perplexed. Addy chuckled. "I can run his picture through photo recognition and get an ID on him."

Jasiah nodded and Maya held his hand once more and squeezed his fingers.

Myles' phone rang. "Sager."

They watched Myles speak for a few moments then he turned to her. "Tate says you should go up to Hickory Hills."

She pulled on Jasiah's hand for him to follow her, but he stood stock-still. "Don't I have to speak to the sheriff about this?"

"Not according to Tate, bud."

Maya looked into his eyes. "Come on Jasiah. Tate will handle things from here. It's more than a local police matter."

He reluctantly followed her from the morgue, and they ascended the steps in silence. Once inside the hospital corridor again, the nurses and staff that had lined the halls waiting to see what happened stepped back and let them pass. No one said anything and they said nothing to anyone else.

Exiting the hospital, she took a deep breath and felt Jasiah's chest expand next to her.

"The air was cloying in there."

He nodded. "It certainly was."

He walked her to his truck, then opened the passenger door for her. Before she stepped in, he pulled her to his body. "I've never been more scared, more nervous, or more proud of anyone in my entire life Maya. You are amazing."

His lips pressed lightly against hers. Her arms slid around his waist and pulled his body to hers tightly. His arms wrapped around her body and circled her in his warmth. Their lips danced together slowly, seductively. His kisses were the stuff of dreams. His body was enticing.

Sirens in the distance broke the spell and he pulled away slightly. "We have to go?"

"Yes. Tate will take care of this in his way."

Jasiah, waited for her to step into his truck, then stepped back and closed the door. He hustled around the front of the truck and climbed in. Maneuvering the truck from the parking lot on the far side, they slipped onto the road and turned up First Road before the sheriff's car turned onto Glenwood.

As they drove, she turned slightly in her seat and faced him. "Do you feel guilty about killing him?"

"Yes. I took a life." She watched his Adam's apple bob and his chest expand as he filled his lungs. "But, he was going to take your life and I won't ever let that happen."

He turned his head and looked into her eyes. "Not ever."

She swallowed the humongous lump that instantly appeared in her throat and took a deep breath to calm her emotions. "I won't ever let anyone hurt you either."

His hand reached out to hers and she gripped it tightly. She'd just sort of declared love to Jasiah. Not in words, but...well, sort of in words. She knew real fear when someone shot at him earlier today. He stood there watching her. Not caring for himself. When had anyone ever done that for her? Not ever. She saw him standing there and yelled and he only watched her.

"Jasiah. The senator told Malibu Man the recording is with the one making changes. You're making changes up here. That's why we think he focused on you. Do you have a recording of some kind?"

His head turned toward her. His brows furrowed before he turned back to the road. "No. I'd have told you if I did."

She watched as the tall brush and trees passed by, the trees soon thinned slightly and the sun started the last half of its setting for the evening. The colors changed from bright oranges and yellows to purples and deep blues. The last section of road turned to gravel, then to dirt as Jasiah parked his truck in the parking area. They sat in the dark, quiet for a few moments. He inhaled deeply and turned to face her. "We didn't get your Jeep."

She smiled. "It's fine. I guess I'll have to spend the night with you."

He chuckled for the first time since this morning. "That's a great idea."

He opened his door and stepped down. As he walked around the front of the truck, his eyes were trained on hers. Her heart skipped several beats as his sensuality sizzled through her. Damn she was lucky.

He opened her door, reached in and grabbed her waist. He pulled her to him and stared into her eyes. "You're incredible, Maya."

She wrapped her arms around his neck and shoulders. The muscles beneath bunched and moved as his hands shimmied up her back. "I think you're pretty incredible, Jasiah."

His head tilted toward hers and his lips softly pressed to hers. His tongue slipped between her lips and danced along her tongue. Their warmth mingled together, their lips molded to each other's perfectly. He pulled away slightly, nipped her lips a few times, then kissed her cheek, then near her ear, below her ear, down her neck, then back up in the same spots.

Goose bumps stood on her arms and down her back, his scent was permanently imprinted in her mind. The feel of his body pressed to hers was all she ever wanted and more. When his lips pressed to hers softly then left she felt the loss as if it were pain.

His eyes held hers for a few beats, then his husky voice broke the silence. "Let's go protect each other again. This time, I get the top."

Her nipples pebbled tightly and the wetness that slammed between her legs damn near made her dizzy. "I can let you have the top." The words barely came out she was so excited.

He pulled her from the truck, set her on the ground,

then took her hand in his and steered them toward his cabin. A few of the residents were outside, gathering firewood or chatting. They smiled as she and Jasiah passed by, he waved and said goodnight. It was real now. They were public. And, truth be told, she was proud as all hell to be with Jasiah Weston. She couldn't wait to tell her mom and Addy about him.

taking his time as he placed another log on the fire. Her bear skin rug comforted her as her dark hair now billowed over her shoulders. Her eyes glistened as the fire roared to life.

He stared into her eyes for a few moments. "Would you like a drink?"

"What do you have? I noticed you don't have a refrigerator."

He glanced around his cabin and back to her. "I suppose this is a first for me, but you're right. I don't have a refrigerator. I've been thinking about all the things I need to change up here now that we have utilities, but I haven't had the chance. But, that can change."

He stood. "I have hard cider."

"Oh, that sounds interesting. I'll try that."

She moved to stand but he shook his head. "Stay right where you are. Let me take care of you tonight."

She settled back on the rug, leaned on her left hand and looked positively gorgeous. He poured them each a cup of hard cider. Then he pulled some bread from a tin his mom had given him and some dried fruit. He arranged them on a plate, opened the lid to another tin and pulled out a pot of honey and set it in the middle of the plate.

Settling on the rug across from her, he set the plate down and handed her a cup of cider. "I made this with my dad and a few others a couple of weeks ago."

She sipped the cider and her brows rose high. "This is good."

She sipped again and he chuckled. "It'll kick you if you aren't careful. So take it slow, baby."

He saw her breath hitch and he cocked his head to the side.

Her cheeks glowed pink. "I like that. When you call me baby. You did it earlier today and all I could think was that I wanted to hear that again and again."

He nodded. "You got it. I was thinking of nicknaming you Helen."

Her shoulders slumped, "Who's that, another old girlfriend?"

He laughed. "Helen of Troy, the most beautiful woman in history. She started the war that brought down a whole empire. This morning when you stood before me naked, I thought you must be Helen of Troy reincarnated. You are incredibly beautiful Maya."

He leaned in and kissed her lips. They were soft and tasted of cider.

He dipped his finger in the honey pot and swiped a thin layer on her bottom lip. He stared into her deep brown eyes and her lips curved up into a sweet, soft smile. He leaned in and kissed her lips. The sweetness of honey, mixed with the cider, and her scent, had his senses whirling. She was intoxicating.

He sat back and licked his lips. She grinned and reached for a piece of bread. "What's your life like up here?"

He glanced around the cabin. "Everything in here is handmade. By either myself or my father. My mom made the quilt on the bed, the placemats for the table, and the curtains. The rug you're sitting on was killed and tanned by me. We work every day up here. Some things have gotten easier as we've brought up the water and electricity. No more walking to the stream to get fresh water. That's been a time saver. But, we live rather simply. I suppose that seems rather backwards to you."

She shook her head. "I live in a beautiful house right now. But, it isn't mine. It's Tate and Lara's. We're allowed rooms and food and equipment as long as we work for GHOST. My parents had their own house even though they both worked for GHOST. Dad had the house first and when they got together, he and mom moved to the base of the mountain. We were always close to GHOST headquarters and mom always kept the room she had there. If they came back late from missions, they'd stay there and come home in the morning. Sometimes as kids we were in the compound and in Mom's room. So, it was easier than waking us up and bringing us home. But, I served in the military and was in a FOB in Afghanistan and that was nothing near as nice as this."

"What's an FOB?"

She chuckled. "It's a Forward Operating Base. We were miles away from base and it was a place to hunker down. We took over an old school and had a roof and rooms and a kitchen. But, it wasn't nice like this. It wasn't homey or made with love. It was necessity and for survival."

"I had no idea."

"Though, I will say, I do love my bathroom down below.

A hot shower does wonders after a long day. Not to mention, shower sex. And, I've never had shower sex, but I hear the others whisper about it."

He whistled low. "Baby, you're making me want to start work on a shower right now."

She laughed. The fire reflected in her dark eyes, and it made her cheeks glow.

She took a deep breath. "We didn't use protection this morning."

He cocked his head to the side. "As in?"

She sat straighter, crossed her legs in front of her and stared into his eyes. "When we had sex. You didn't use a condom."

"I don't have any."

"What do you use up here if you don't want to get pregnant?"

"We pull out."

"You didn't pull out either."

They stared for a long time, neither saying anything. The thoughts swirled through his mind at her words. "No."

"Is that the only protection you have up here?"

"Yes."

"So, you always pulled out?"

"Yes. Baby, there isn't a child up here that looks like me. And, in case you haven't noticed, there aren't a ton of women who are available either."

She nodded and swallowed. "But you didn't pull out this morning."

His voice lowered. "No."

Her head cocked to the side as she stared into his eyes. "Jasiah." She swallowed.

He leaned in and kissed her lips once more. She tilted her head to fit their lips together and her tongue slid into his mouth. His hand held the back of her head so their lips stayed together. He softened his kiss to mold his lips to hers sweetly. His mind whirled by their words and she was right, he didn't pull out. It had been drilled into him from the time he was ten years old that he never, ever, let himself go in a woman until he was ready to make a child. And, yet this morning, that thought did not even so much as knock on his brain. Not once. Not even throughout the day had he thought of it.

[illegible] showed his [illegible] this afternoon [illegible] but now it was time to [illegible] love and [illegible]. She was all for that.

Their lips danced and molded together perfectly. The honey he'd spread on her bottom lip helped that somewhat [illegible]. More than she'd have thought he could ever be. He was a mountain man. Rugged and brawny. This tender side was a revelation and she liked that she was experiencing another layer of Jasiah.

He pulled away from her and began unbuttoning his shirt. Her eyes locked on his fingers as he undid each button. He swallowed once and she watched his Adam's apple bob. He pulled his arms free of his shirt, and laid it on the rug farthest from the fireplace.

Deliberately he picked up the plate between them and set it on the table, before moving their cups of cider to the fireplace hearth.

When he turned to her, his eyes danced, the fine lines at the corners crinkled slightly as his smile grew.

He reached an arm out and slid her to him, then gently pushed her back to the rug, his hand protectively behind her head. Hovering over her, he slowly lowered himself so he was half on top, and half to the side, but his eyes never left hers. Goose bumps skittered across her body, the hair on her arms rose. It wasn't from the cold, she'd never been so warm.

He swallowed again and she reached up and traced her forefinger along his Adam's apple, then down the middle of his chest, until their bodies pressed together halted her progress. His left hand snuck under her t-shirt and smoothed across her abdomen. The roughness of his hand sent a riot of shivers in its wake. His finger wiggled under her bra and his hand molded over her right breast and squeezed gently. His thumb swiped over her nipple and the electricity that zipped through her and landed between her legs nearly took her breath away. She squirmed under his touch, but her eyes never left his.

Her hands shimmied down her body and unfastened her slacks. She still had her boots on, and started to lift herself to untie them. He gently pushed on her chest.

"I'll do it," he husked.

He kissed her lips gently then sat up and reached for her feet. Taking her left foot in his hands, he lifted her leg slightly, untied her boot and slid it from her foot. Her sock followed. He slowly repeated his motions on her right foot.

He sat up on his knees, placed his hands on either side of her hips, and tugged her slacks down her hips, legs, and pulled them from her body, laying them at her feet.

She shimmied out of her long-sleeved t-shirt and set it alongside.

He whispered, "Helen."

Her cheeks heated but goosebumps formed on her arms. Opposite emotions at the same time. It was a head rush.

His work-roughened hands smoothed up her body, stopping at her panties. He leaned down and kissed her naval, then lower, he kissed across the elastic where her panties covered her body. He tucked his thumbs into her panties from the bottom, then curved his fingers and tugged them down her legs.

"So beautiful," he breathed.

His lips kissed her clit, softly, gently. He peppered kisses all around, driving her insane with want. Finally his tongue slid up her center and sucked in her clit. Breath escaped her lungs; her legs parted; and her hands dove into his hair. His thick, soft, beautiful hair.

His tongue drove her wild, circling, licking, nipping. Using one hand he unzipped his pants, pushed them over his hips, never leaving her body with his mouth.

It took some time. She grinned a few times, because she certainly would have helped him divest of his clothing. But, he was determined to do this his way.

Finally, he moved his kisses higher, across her belly, under her breasts, over her nipples, sucking each one in separately, his opposite hand massaged the other in time.

Once he'd given equal attention to both breasts, his lips sought hers once more. His body settled between her legs, his erection laying on her near her entrance, his arms held her on either side.

She spread her legs open further and he lifted slightly, positioned himself at her entrance and slowly slid himself inside. Her eyes closed as she mentally imprinted this feeling on her brain. She'd relive this feeling over and over again in her lifetime. It was magnificent.

He groaned as he pulled out and slowly entered her again. Her eyes opened to see his deep, rich brown eyes staring at her. He laid on his elbows, his hands sought each of hers and held them slightly above her head as he entered her again and again.

The firelight danced in his eyes, making him look other-worldly. He was everything.

His pace increased and she felt her orgasm build, her hips met his move for move.

"Jasiah..." she huffed out softly.

"Maya." He pushed in again. "Should I pull out?"

She raised her hips again, meeting him solidly, eager for her orgasm. One more time and she'd be there.

He pushed in solidly. She gasped and strained as her orgasm flew through her like the fire they lay before. Hot pleasure screamed through her body.

His kissed her lips and brought her back to this world. "In or out." He commanded.

She stared into his eyes, her fingers squeezed his tightly. "In."

He pushed twice more, the muscles in his body tensed, his eyes took on another look of pure pleasure as he poured himself into her. They froze as they were, staring at each other. The meaning of what just happened washed over her in a flood of pure emotion and elation. She was in love with Jasiah Weston and she wasn't concerned if she'd just gotten pregnant. In fact, she'd love to fill this cabin with many of his babies.

A tear trickled down the side of her face to her temple. He kissed the tear away, his lips near her ear, his voice husky and gruff, as he said, "I love you, Maya Sager."

on his ceiling.
wrapped around her, her naked
against him.

She stirred, stretched, and tilted her head to look into his eyes. "Morning."

He grinned. Her sleepiness was adorable. "Good

"I have to pee."

He chuckled. "I'll make you some tea while you go."

She glanced around the cabin. "Where would that be?"

"I have a chamber pot in the corner." He pointed to the curtains that separated his bedroom from the main cabin. He'd never pulled them closed, there'd never been need.

"Or," she sighed.

"There's an outhouse behind the garden."

She kissed his lips quickly, sat up and began dressing. "I'm opting for the outhouse."

"Okay," he husked. His heart dropped a little. He couldn't

offer her what she had down below. He could make improvements though.

He stood and stretched, then grabbed his briefs and pulled them on. Maya's hands smoothed up his back and circled around his waist. Her hands brushed along his chest, then her arms tightened and squeezed him tightly to her. Her cheek pressed into his back, his arms felt empty. He reached back and squeezed her as much as he could.

Her arms loosened and he turned. Filling his lungs with air, he let it out slowly. His heartbeat sped up. His life changed dramatically in a short week's time. So much promise for the future, loss speeding toward him as fast as a freight train. He pressed his lips to hers and emotion slammed him in the chest.

She stepped back. "Gotta pee. I'll be right back."

Swallowing, he inhaled a couple of deep breaths as she stepped into the crisp morning air.

He quickly made the bed, something that had been drilled into him from the time he could do it. Get out of bed and make it before you do anything else. Once that was finished, he filled his tea kettle with water and hung it on the cast iron arm and swung it into the fireplace.

Pulling wood from the rack near the fireplace, he lay kindling and three logs in the cooling fireplace, struck his Ferro stick a few times and started the kindling on fire. He blew a couple times to grow the fire, then sat back and made sure it started the logs to burning.

Preparing two cups for tea, scooping tea into the infusers, he glanced out the window to see the community beginning to wake up.

Maya stepped into the front door, pulled her jacket off and hung it on the empty wooden hook next to his jacket.

A smile grew across his face. She turned and cocked her head. "What?"

"I like your jacket next to mine."

She laughed. "Okay."

She pulled her cell phone from her pocket. "I need your phone number please."

"You need it?"

Her eyes danced and her lips parted in a gorgeous smile. "I need it bad."

He laughed. "Okay. I need your number too."

Maya stepped toward him and kissed his lips. He pulled his phone out of his pocket and gave Maya his number. Her fingers flew over her phone and his phone chimed a text from her.

He read the text and grinned.

> "Reply to this and I'll have your number.
> Last night was wonderful."

He tapped a reply,

> "Helen."

The smile that grew on her face was stunning. She sent back a heart.

He stepped forward and pulled her in for a hug, his heartbeat was erratic and it was because of her.

The whistle on the teapot blew, and Jasiah stepped back and lifted it from the hook. He poured the water into each cup, dropped in the infusers and set the kettle on the hook.

"What's going on today?" He asked.

"Well, I need to get my Jeep. Check in at home and see what Tate has in store for me today. But, first, I'll stand in the shower for a bit and ruminate on last night."

He chuckled. "I'll be ruminating on last night for years to come."

She chuckled. "Me too."

He lifted the infuser from his teacup and sipped the hot liquid. "I have bread, eggs, and honey. Should I make you some breakfast before we go down the mountain?"

"I have a confession to make." She pulled her hair into a ponytail. "I don't cook."

"I didn't ask you to cook for me. I offered to cook for you."

"Yeah, but I thought I should let you know, I can't cook. I shoot, and run, and research, and a host of other things. Cooking is not one of them."

"You were cooking pretty good last night." He kissed her lips. She giggled. "So were you."

He stepped back. "I told you last night that I love you. I meant that. And, I've never said it to anyone before. We'll work out the cooking thing. We've got a couple of women up here who are feeling displaced with folks utilizing modern conveniences and going down the mountain to work. I'll bet we could pay them to cook for us."

"I can pay for food. That eases my mind a bit. I'd hate to have you hungry all the time."

A laugh burst from his chest. "Okay. That's taken care of. Let's eat, I'll cook, then we'll get you down the mountain."

"Okay. I can set the table."

"Thank you."

He reached into the wooden box on the counter and pulled out three eggs. Maya pulled plates off the shelf above the sink and set them on the placemats.

"How can you keep eggs without a refrigerator?"

"We don't wash them. That keeps the bloom intact and

they don't require cooling. We've never had refrigeration up here, so that's how we've always kept them."

"Wow. I never knew."

"Stick with me, you'll learn a lot."

She laughed and he stopped slicing the bread to stare at her. She made life great.

____

She [let the water wash over her. She] [rel]axed and turned the water temperature up.

Spending a bit more time than usual in the shower, she dried her hair, dressed, and ventured out to see who was around and what was going on today.

Tate and Myles were in the kitchen, finishing breakfast. Myles added, "There she is. She was about to sleep up."

She shot him a dirty look and kept moving toward the refrigerator. "Good morning to you as well."

Tate stood and huffed out a breath. "Maya, when you have a moment, I need to speak with you."

"Sounds good. I'll be in as soon as I grab a cup of coffee."

She prepared her coffee, took a sip and closed her eyes as the hot liquid slid down her throat. "Ahh," she whispered.

Taking a deep breath she turned to Myles. "Go ahead, get it out of your system."

"Get what out of my system?"

"Jasiah."

She leaned her hip against the counter, held her cup in front of her and leveled her eyes on his.

"You think it's a phase?"

"Is it?"

"No."

"Really?"

"Really. I love him, Myles. He loves me."

Myles stared at her for a while. His emotions played across his face. His chest expanded and he let out a deep breath. "Okay."

She sauntered to the table and sat in the chair next to her brother. Placing her coffee cup on the table, she turned her chair to face him.

"I love him." She swallowed. "I've never been in love before. It's exciting and new and scary."

"You live different lives."

"I'm so very aware of that. As I walked to the outhouses this morning, my thoughts ran wild. There are obstacles. He won't live down here. He's their leader. His life is up there."

"Your life is down here."

"What's down here that keeps me from living up there?"

Myles' head dropped slightly. She continued. "I have a phone. Jasiah has a phone. I can be down here in fifteen minutes if something happens. I can still do my job. Mom and Dad lived off-site and still did their jobs."

Myles swallowed heavily. "Yeah."

His eyes lifted to hers. "Are you sure?"

"That I love him? Yes. We haven't talked about anything beyond that. I've just been thinking about it and what could possibly happen."

"I've only lived away from you in the military. We've always been together."

She chuckled. "Yeah. But, eventually you'll get married and I don't see us all living together. Do you?"

"Fuck no."

"Okay. You're my brother. My twin. We are connected in ways that no other person on earth can understand except another twin. That will never change."

"Yeah. I love you Maya and want you happy." He grinned. "I also want to be in the room when you tell Mom you want to live up on the mountain."

She shook her head. "I didn't say I wanted to. I may have to. And, believe me, I've been thinking about telling Mom. I'm not sure what the reaction will be."

"Like I said, I want to be in the room."

"We'll see." She stood. "I've got to see Tate. Wanna have lunch today?"

"Sure."

She leaned down and kissed the top of Myles' head. Turned and exited the kitchen with her coffee cup.

Tapping on Tate's door, he called out, "Come on in, Maya."

She grinned. He knew the sound of their footsteps.

She pushed the door open and stepped in.

Tate turned from his computers. "Please run down for me what happened at the morgue yesterday. Then, I need to speak to Jasiah. I have to report all of this to Rafe."

She chuckled. "It'll take a little bit to hear Rafe and not Casper."

"Believe me, it's taken me a bit to say Rafe and not Casper."

She told him what happened at the morgue and that Malibu Man had turned to shoot her when Jasiah shot him. Tate nodded, didn't take notes, but watched her closely.

That's what he did. She'd learned not to be worried about that.

"Okay. I'll be calling Jasiah soon and asking him to come in."

"Sounds good."

She stood to leave and Tate asked, "It's none of my business as your boss, but as your friend, are you and Jasiah together?"

Her smile felt impossibly big. It was hard not to when she thought of Jasiah. "Yes. We're together."

Tate grinned. "Good for you. I've dealt with him over these past two years and he's a stand-up man."

"I think so too."

"Myles okay with it?"

"Yeah. He's good. We're good Tate."

He nodded. "That's good to hear."

"Also, Jasiah doesn't have a recording of any kind. Where do we look from here?"

"I'll think on it a bit and speak with Rafe."

She stepped from his office and headed toward Addy's room. Then she'd call her mom and see if they'd come down and meet Jasiah. It was surreal, all these new things and the getting to know the family. But, almost the instant she'd seen Jasiah kneeling in the woods, something in her just knew he was the man she'd waited for her whole life. It's like her soul told her he's the one.

Her phone rang before she reached Addy's door. Jasiah's name appeared on her screen. She'd need to get a picture of him.

"Hi." Her smile grew as she turned and headed toward her room.

"Hi. I just got a call from Tate. He wants to speak to me about the morgue. Is everything alright?"

"Yeah. He has a report to write up and he has to speak to each of us. That was his promise to the sheriff, who I guess was happy to not have to write up the report. Plus, Casp...Rafe needs it for his files."

"Okay. It's going to take me a bit, I have a few things to take care of up here first. Do you want to have lunch later?"

"I do. But, Myles already asked to have lunch with me. How about all three of us have lunch?"

"That sounds great. It's time I meet him in a casual manner I guess."

"That it is. See you in a while."

had ever been.

A buzzer sounded and the gates slid open. He moved [illegible] on his phone screen.

"Hey, there."

She giggled and it was cute. "Hi. Pull around to the back of the building. I have my garage door open and you can park behind the Jeep."

"Okay. See you in a minute."

He navigated the corner and saw her standing there. The sun shone on her hair, pulled up in her customary ponytail. She wore a long dark orange sweater and jeans today. She still had her tactical boots on, but then again, that was her.

Her smile was like coming home. It beamed at him and his heart beat a bit faster seeing her. He hoped this feeling would never go away.

He jumped from his truck and scooped her up in his arms the second she was close enough. He kissed her lips, her feet still dangling.

"It's good to see you again."

She giggled. "It's good to see you."

He set her down and she took his hand and led him through the garage. "So, this is the garage, obviously. But, we also have a workout room over there..." She pointed to the right. "And a shooting range over there." She pointed to the left.

"Indoor gun range? That's impressive."

"It's nice to have here. We practice at least three times a week. It's a job requirement."

"Perfectly understandable."

At the door he leaned forward to open it, but it swung open from inside. Myles stood in the doorway, his face unreadable. That's likely what made him a great operative.

"Hi, Jasiah. Welcome to the HOG."

"Thank you. What's the HOG?"

He lifted his hands in the air, "This. Home. Office. Garage. The HOG."

He grinned and Jasiah leaned forward to shake his hand, which Myles shook immediately.

Maya winked at him and it did things to his body. Specifically, a shiver skittered down his spine, circled around, and landed in his favorite spot.

Myles stepped back to allow them entry. "I understand we'll be having lunch together today."

Jasiah nodded. "I'm looking forward to it."

Maya took his hand again. "What do you want to do first, get a tour or speak with Tate?"

"I'd love the tour, but think I should speak with Tate first. It's been a couple of hours since he called and I don't think it's right to keep him waiting."

Maya's smile was sweet. "You're a good man, Jasiah."

He nodded even as his cheeks warmed. "I was raised to be nothing less."

He nodded to Myles, "I'll see you in a bit."

Myles nodded in return and Maya tugged his hand and moved them through the kitchen. He managed to look around a bit as he moved through the room. It was a beautiful home Maya lived in. A knot formed in his throat and ugly doubts crept inside. He focused on her hand in his and her smile when she turned her head to look at him.

She knocked on a partially open door, "Tate, Jasiah's here."

"Come on in, Jasiah."

Maya nodded for him to go inside, and she waved at him as she turned to leave.

He wasn't in trouble, but he sure felt as though he had done something wrong. Myles' assessment had been laying there, underneath the greeting. And, that could just be his own guilt for having slept with Maya, and not pulled out, before making any kind of proper declaration. He should have learned that from Zara. Though, he pulled out, he never made a declaration to her family of any kind and that has been a lingering pain in the ass for eight damned years.

"I'm not sure if Maya told you, but I have a report to complete, and I feel that I need to be thorough. Rafe is in his new position, Casper is dealing with matters of the utmost importance, and I want to make sure we have all of our I's dotted and T's crossed."

"I understand."

"Okay." Tate sat at his desk, his hands folded in front of him, and his eyes focused on him. It was a bit unnerving. As if he was being assessed. "Tell me what happened at the morgue. Before, during, and after."

Jasiah took his time recalling the details of that day. He especially focused on the man looking at Maya as he pointed his gun and the fear that roared down his spine. He felt he had no choice but to protect her. In all, his meeting with Tate lasted close to an hour.

Tate nodded. "Thank you for coming in, Jasiah. Just one last question."

"Okay."

"Are you alright? I can get you help if you need it. It isn't easy taking a life. Sometimes there are lingering aftereffects that can rear up."

Jasiah leaned forward and looked into Tate's blue eyes. "I'm fine, Tate. I appreciate you asking, but if I had to do it again, I'd do it a thousand times to save Maya."

Tate nodded. "I've noticed that not once did you mention fear for yourself."

Jasiah's brows bunched for a moment. He sat back in his seat. "I never felt fear for myself, I guess. I only worried Maya would be hurt."

Tate nodded. "Thank you. I'm happy you've found each other."

Jasiah stood and leaned forward to shake Tate's hand. "Thank you, Tate. I appreciate it."

"What's happening with the election?"

"Tonight I have to address the community and tell them some ideas I have for moving forward. After lunch I have a meeting with the mayor, then I'll go up and get ready."

"Good luck with that, Jasiah. You're a great leader, I hope your people see that."

He grinned. "I hope so too, but I have options if they don't."

M[illegible] on her [illegible] the place. [illegible] noting that Josiah had been in [illegible] late for [illegible] hours. Blowing out a breath, she called her mom.

"Hi, honey. How are you?"

"I'm good, Mom. How are you and Dad?"

"We're good. Isi was just telling me about Rafe and how Addly is just a l'il love bug. They all like Rafe. And feel good about their marriage."

"Rafe's a good guy. He has a monumental task ahead of him taking over for Casper, but he seems to be handling it well."

"That's what Josh said. How's Myles?"

"He's good. Have you spoken to him recently?"

"Not for a few days. Is everything alright?"

She cleared her throat. "I met someone. And, by someone, I mean THE one. I met him."

Her mom let out a breath. She could hear movement in the background and her breathing changed.

"Okay. I'm in the office with your father. Tell us about this man you met."

She smiled thinking of Jasiah. "Hi, Dad." She took a breath, "His name is Jasiah Weston. He's the president in Hickory Hills. He's smart. Strong. Fun to be around. He makes me happy."

Her dad cleared his throat. "He's with the BRR?"

Her voice was forceful, "The BRR doesn't exist any longer. At least as a whole. There are a few of Craig's followers left up there, but the majority of the community likes the direction they're moving in and that is in partnership with Glen Hollow, not in opposition. Many of them have secured jobs down here. They have water, electricity, and gas up on the mountain now. Homes are being retrofitted to embrace the new utilities. The talk up there is now how to better merge with Glen Hollow, not wipe them out."

"Okay. I'm sorry. I didn't mean to make you mad."

She settled back on the bar stool and let her shoulders relax. "I'm sorry. I just wanted you to know that while he's Craig's nephew, he's nothing like Craig."

"Thank God for that," her mom said.

"Yeah."

Her mom's voice softened. "When can we meet him, Maya?"

"When can you come down here?"

"What about Thanksgiving? A few of us thought it would be fun to have a family Thanksgiving and come and join you. Aidyn and Elena were talking about coming down now that the danger seems to be passed. They'd like everyone to meet Teagan too."

"Oh, that sounds fantastic. I'd love that. All of that."

Her mom chuckled. "We'd love that too. Let's plan it. It's only a week away."

"Okay. Why don't you all talk about what's going to happen and when. Then, ask Sophie to coordinate with Tate and Lara."

"That sounds good, honey. We'll see you in a week. I love you."

"I love you too, Mom. Dad, I love you."

"I love you baby girl."

She waited for them to end the call, then set her phone on the counter.

"What's happening and when?"

She whirled around to see Myles standing behind her, a grin on his face.

"Mom, Dad, Gaige, Sophie, Aidyn and Elena, and the rest of the crew are coming here for Thanksgiving."

"Really? Wow, that's fantastic."

"It's exciting. It'll be such a fun Thanksgiving."

Jasiah entered the kitchen at that time. "An exciting Thanksgiving?"

"Mom and Dad and the whole GHOST crew are planning on coming here for Thanksgiving. Including Aidyn and Elena."

Jasiah's brows rose into the air. "Really? Oh, there are a lot of people up there who'd love to see Elena again."

"That's what I was thinking. And, they had a baby. Teagan. They're bringing her too. We've never met her."

Jasiah's smile was beautiful. "Wow, that's something. I'll make sure to tell my mom. She liked Elena very much."

Maya's stomach knotted. She'd never been a jealous type of person. She was more self-assured than anyone. But hearing Jasiah's mom liked Elena, who had been a single woman up on the mountain, had her wondering if she wanted Elena as a daughter-in-law.

Myles clapped his hands. "I'm hungry. Are you two ready to go?"

Jasiah nodded, "Absolutely."

Maya got off her stool, closed her laptop and picked it up. "I have to put my laptop away. Let me show you around a bit, Jasiah. Then we can go."

She walked past Jasiah. He turned and followed her to her room. "So this is my room." She set her laptop into its case on the foot of her bed. "I have a sofa to sit on, my bed of course, and this is my bathroom over here." She stepped into the bathroom and flipped the light switch.

Jasiah stepped inside and looked around. "This is amazing."

"It's pretty nice."

"What's your favorite thing about it?"

She looked into his eyes, then waved her hand in front of the shower. "This."

The tiled shower with a large shower head stood between the door and the toilet. The sink was alongside the shower. Not a huge room but very nice.

"I can see how shower sex would be fun in here."

She looked into his eyes, there was humor in them. The lines at the corners of his eyes stood out as he grinned. "Yeah. Me too. If Myles wasn't waiting for us, we could see for ourselves."

His arms snaked out and pulled her close. His lips landed on hers with the passion she enjoyed from him. Her tongue dipped into his mouth, her hands grabbed his shirt and held on as he made love to her mouth with his.

When he pulled back she whispered, "That did nothing to erase shower sex from my mind."

"I didn't mean it too, baby. I meant to cement it in your mind. We'll absolutely have shower sex."

"Fantastic," she whispered.

He pecked her lips again, then stepped back. "Myles is waiting for us."

"Yeah. Myles."

She grinned, stepped from the room and waited for Jasiah as he flipped the switch off after one last glance.

...toward the kitchen, then nodded. "Yes."

"Great. Let's go in there."

...following behind. He didn't sit once in the kitchen, in fact he seemed in a hurry.

"I just got word from Casper. The president-elect has gone missing. Of course, he has secret service protection, so it's quite puzzling as to where he is. Secret service doesn't know what happened."

Maya spoke first. "That's incredible. Do you think it's a made-up story?"

Tate pointed to her briefly then tucked his hands in his front pockets. "That's what I wondered. And, of course, we know from the senator and the documents he had, that there are many corrupt people in D.C. So if he wanted to bribe someone to help him, he'd not find it too hard to find someone to take a bribe. For all we know, someone on the inside was also in the know of the Yerezdan deals and was easy to blackmail."

Jasiah couldn't help but thinking how horribly corrupt this government had become. In so many ways they were still so pure up in Hickory Hills despite the war that led them up there and the events that transpired. Once separated, they had their own leadership, which had spoiled. They had the chance at a fresh start now and he'd work hard to make the people know how terrible this government had become to get to this point. Hopefully, they'd stave off the treachery up there. Hopefully.

Myles scoffed. "So, do you think he'd come here?"

Tate shrugged. "I don't know. Rafe and Casper are still hashing out some details, but no one seems to know where he's gone. On the one hand, I don't see what coming here would do for him. Unless he thinks the recording is here. On the other hand, he might not be thinking straight and shooting from the hip. He was told last night about Lee Hombs."

Maya asked, "Who's that?"

Tate grinned. "You called him Malibu Man. Lee Hombs was an aide in Senator Jackson's office. He worked closely with the senator. He knew all about the corruption and what the senator had done for King. Apparently when the senator went into hiding, Hombs contacted King and worked a deal. He'd get the papers for King for a million dollars and safe passage out of the country."

Maya nodded. "So that was King's last chance to try to destroy the papers and make this all go away."

"It appears that way." Tate shrugged. "Be careful. Be watchful. We don't know where King is, and we don't know if he's already found someone else to finish the job Hombs didn't finish."

Maya looked up at him. She took his hand in hers. "Will you reconsider staying down here for protection?"

He stared into her eyes but shook his head. "I cannot do that to my people. If there's danger up there and I leave them alone, I'm not the leader they'll want. Nor will they think of me as anything but a coward. I'm not a coward."

"Jasiah..."

"I won't change my mind, Maya. I can't."

Myles stepped forward. "I volunteer to go up there for protection."

He stared at Myles. His eyes mirrored his sisters and this time when he looked in them, he didn't see judgment. "Thank you, Myles. I don't want anyone putting themselves in harm's way for me."

"It would be for my sister," Myles ticked. "She loves you. So, it would be for her. And you."

Jasiah swallowed the lump in his throat. He didn't have siblings. But, he'd do the same if he had them. "Thank you, Myles."

Maya nodded. "I'll volunteer as well."

Spencer entered the room. "What are you volunteering for?"

Myles nodded toward him. "We're volunteering to be on protection duty for Hickory Hills in case King sends someone else up there to finish the job Malibu Man didn't finish."

Spencer nodded. "I'll volunteer for that too."

Tate grinned. "You all are a dream team for sure. Jasiah, here's your protection team."

He shook his head, that lump still in his throat. Sucking in a deep breath, he nodded. "Thank you all."

He tugged Maya's hand and moved her closer. His arm slid around her shoulders and he kissed the top of her head. "I'm a lucky man."

Spencer grinned. "Yeah, I admit it, she's something special."

Maya chuckled. "I knew you'd admit it one day."

Spencer laughed out loud. "I've said it plenty. So, what's the plan?"

Jasiah swallowed. "I have to address the community tonight to tell them what I have planned for future expansion. It's sort of my presidential speech, I guess. I don't know if my opposition will be there, I assume he will be. But, I don't think he's violent."

Myles stepped toward the door. "Okay. So, we'll be on the perimeter making sure no one approaches from the woods."

Jasiah nodded. "Thank you. Though I don't know why they'd come up there looking for me."

Maya glanced up at him. "At this point, it could just be because you killed Malibu Man."

Jasiah looked at Tate. "Does everyone know who killed him?"

"Not that I'm aware of. Though, King had all night to send out feelers to find out what happened."

"No one knew but us."

"Hospital staff may have found out. There are cameras down there."

Jasiah closed his eyes for a moment and nodded.

Myles broke the silence that followed. "I'm hungry."

Tate and Spencer laughed. Jasiah chuckled and squeezed Maya's shoulders. "Let's go eat." Nodding to Tate and Spencer, "Thank you. I appreciate your concern."

Myles glanced at Spencer. "We're going to lunch. I'll find you when we return and we'll discuss when to go up and what we'll do."

Spencer waved. "Have a great lunch."

34

M[illegible] to the [illegible] Jasiah had a [illegible] and at least to her, it seemed that Myles learned to respect Jasiah as a man. That was important to her. And, of course, Myles would be chatting with their parents, and she wanted him to confirm to her parents that Jasiah was a good man.

After loading up her Jeep, she left Brookswood and headed toward Glass Hollow. She'd packed a bag just for an overnight stay. A toothbrush and deodorant. She'd make do with a sink bath occasionally and the outhouse. As long as she had clean clothes and deodorant, she'd feel better.

She rolled her window down and let her hair blow in the wind. It was a crisp fall day, but it felt good. Life felt good right now.

Turning up Last Road, she slowed around the corners and slammed on her brakes when she saw Marni duck into a thicket of brush.

She jumped from her Jeep and ran around to the other side of the road.

"Marni. It's me, Maya."

Maya stepped into the thicket of brush she'd seen Marni dive into and pushed at the thick brush with her hands. She stepped over a downed log, and tripped on thick brush. Lifting her head, she saw Marni watching her.

"Hey, why are you running from me?"

Marni shrugged. "I don't know."

Maya untangled herself from the long brush that grabbed and scratched her. Some of that brush had thorns.

"Are you alright?"

Marni shrugged. "Yeah."

Maya stopped in front of her. "The other day when I came to your house and asked you if you'd seen anyone else, you seemed to hesitate before answering. If you were afraid to say something in front of your mom, you can tell me now. I won't say anything to your mom, but it sure might help me. And Jasiah."

Marni shook her head. "My dad doesn't like Jasiah."

"I know. Do you know why?"

Marni shrugged. "Something to do with my mom and Craig."

"Okay."

Marni looked around the woods as if to see if someone was listening. "I didn't tell the truth."

"About what honey?"

She took a deep breath. "I did see someone."

"Okay. Who did you see?"

"That man. Before he killed the senator, I saw him in the woods."

"Can you show me where you saw him?"

Marni turned and made her way across the uneven floor of the woods. She easily jumped over downed logs and brush. She stopped before a small copse of trees. "He was hiding in here."

Maya stepped to the copse of trees and peered inside. "Did you see what he was doing?"

"Sleeping."

"Okay." Maya stepped into the copse and felt around the ground for anything that might be of use.

Marni then said, "Why do you care?"

Maya sat back on her haunches. "It's my job to bring the man who killed the senator to justice. In actuality, the man who shot him, killed him. But, in the bigger picture, someone hired him to do that and we want to get that man. So anything you saw, picked up, or have that might lead me to that bad man, will really help us. It'll help a lot of people too. Because he's bad and needs to be in jail for all the bad things he's done."

"Okay." Marni toed the ground and tucked her hands in her pockets. Maya waited her out, hoping she had something to offer. Anything.

After a long silence, Maya began sweeping her hands over the ground once more, then sat back when she found nothing. "Okay. I appreciate you telling me Marni. I've got to get up to Jasiah. I'll see you later tonight, okay?"

"Okay." Maya fought her way back to her Jeep and climbed in. She turned to her right to see if she could still see Marni in the woods, but she couldn't. She should have offered her a ride, but that girl spent a ton of time in the woods, so she'd likely not have taken it anyway. But, she should have offered. Pushing away the guilt, she took a deep breath and started her Jeep.

Navigating three more corners before reaching the last parking area, Maya turned her Jeep off and jumped out.

Opening the back door, she pulled her bags from inside and lugged them to Jasiah's cabin. She knocked on the door but he didn't answer. Twisting the knob, the door opened so she stepped inside and dragged her bags in. She had one more bag to bring in.

She trudged across the side of the common area, reached her Jeep and pulled the last bag and her duffle bag from inside. She closed the door to Jasiah's cabin and started unpacking her bags.

She smiled from ear to ear as she unboxed and placed things around the cabin. She had never been a domestic type of gal. It was laughable even now that she was doing this. Her mom would get a huge kick out of this. She was getting a huge kick out of this.

The door opened and Jasiah stood in the door with a grin on his face. "What's all this?"

She turned and plopped her hands on her hips. "Honey, I need coffee in the morning. So, I bought you a coffee maker. Then I bought creamer for said coffee, and several kinds of coffee since you liked the one I brought you. Then, I thought, wouldn't it be nice to have some of Lara's cookies with our coffee, so I bought some of those. Then..."

Jasiah crossed the room and laughed. "Stop." He kissed her lips. She held onto his shoulders then slid her arms around his waist and pulled his body close. "I love that we'll have coffee in the morning."

"And cookies."

He laughed. "And cookies."

She kissed him again and enjoyed the feel of his lips on hers. She mumbled around their kisses. "I hate shopping, so this is big Jasiah. I must really love you."

He chuckled. "I'm happy to hear that."

A soft knock on the door had Jasiah pulling away, his brows furrowed. He opened the door to Marni. She watched Jasiah look back and forth.

"What are you doing here Marni? Is everything alright?"

She swallowed and looked around Jasiah to her. "I wasn't honest."

Maya stepped toward the little girl and knelt down. "About what?"

Marni pulled her hand from her pocket and in it was a thumb drive. "He had this."

Maya gently took it from her hand. "Do you know what this is?"

Marni shook her head.

Maya turned the thumb drive over in her hand. "Who had this, Marni?"

"The senator."

Maya's brows rose into her bangs. "The senator had this? Did he say what it was for?"

"He said it was the final proof to bring down the president."

"Oh. Okay." Maya tucked it in her back pocket. "Did he give it to you?"

"Yeah. He asked me if I could keep a secret. I nodded and he handed it to me."

"Why did you hide it?"

Marni's eyes slid to Jasiah's. "I didn't want to bring down Jasiah."

Maya choked back a sob. This little girl held a big secret and was afraid of what it meant. "Ohh." Maya swallowed the lump in her throat. "Oh, honey. He didn't mean this president, Jasiah. He meant the new president of the United States."

Marni's blue eyes searched hers for a long time. "Okay." She looked up at Jasiah, then back to her.

"Am I in trouble?"

Maya shook her head. "No, honey, you aren't in trouble."

"Don't tell my dad." Her voice cracked slightly.

"We won't tell your dad."

35

"You know I have to give a speech in about a half hour. I can't have you looking at me like you'd like to have your way with me."

She laughed. "I always want to have my way with you. But, I can't help how I look at you."

He stepped into his jeans and reached across the table for his shirt. She grabbed it before he could and tugged on it.

He locked eyes with her and moved toward her slowly. The instant he stood before her, she set her coffee on the hearth next to her and slowly pulled his jeans open. Her small fingers pulled his briefs down to expose his cock. Dipping her beautiful head down, she kissed along the length of him, which grew thicker by the second.

Maya shimmied his jeans over his hips. She tugged his briefs down and her mouth sucked in his cock slowly. The warmth of her mouth around him made his knees weak. He reached for the mantle above her and held himself up with both hands. Maya's hands cupped his balls and his cock as her warm, wet mouth sucked him fully. She swirled her tongue across his tip, then sucked him in again.

His breathing came in short shudders as his balls tightened. Her fingers massaged his tightened balls and her mouth continued to bring him closer to ecstasy. His hips moved as his orgasm raged forward, her sucking grew in intensity, the sensations running through his body were overwhelming. His balls drew up tightly and he couldn't get her name to come out of his mouth because his breathing couldn't keep up with the sensations she heaped on him.

With a loud groan, his orgasm released in spurts, her hands softened on his cock, her tongue lapped at him until he was finished.

He lay his head on his right arm, as he focused on not falling to the ground. His legs still shook as his mind reeled.

Slowly and gently, Maya pulled up his briefs, tucking him in gently. His jeans came next. Her hands cupped his ass before sliding the jeans over it. When she had them in place as he'd been before, she grinned up at him. "Now I think you're relaxed and ready to go out there and talk to your community."

He stared at her for a moment, then squatted in front of her. "You're sassy."

"Get used to it."

"God. That is something I can't wait to get used to." He kissed her lips softly, then stood and buttoned his jeans, zipped them up and picked up her coffee cup and took a sip before handing it back to her.

She giggled, "I guess we can call that fireplace sex."

He chuckled. "I guess we can. Next time, it's your turn."

"Yes, please." Her lips parted into the most beautiful smile.

Filling his lungs with air, he slipped his shirt on. "Tell me what you'll be doing while I'm addressing the community."

"Myles, Spencer, and I will be patrolling the perimeter of the common area. Henry, Addy, and Tate will be watching the cameras from below to make sure no one comes up the roads."

"Okay." He buttoned his shirt. "And after?"

"And, after, Myles and Spencer will go to the HOG and they'll work around the clock watching the cameras. I'll be here with you."

She stood and closed the distance between them. "We aren't going to let anything happen to you."

"We don't even know they want to harm me."

"It seems Malibu Man focused on you for a reason. Since Marni had a thumb drive, we know why now. When he shot the senator, he wanted to get out of there in case we'd already called the police. I'm assuming he felt he'd come back and find the recording and finish the job. And, he likely had contact with King or his men in the process and likely offered your name."

"Why isn't he after you then?"

"We don't know he isn't. That's why I'm up here with you." She stood on her toes and lightly pecked his lips. "That and other reasons."

"I like the other reasons." He kissed her quickly, squeezed her tightly, and stepped back. "Okay, I have to meet with Reece and the men before I address the community."

"You'll do an excellent job, Jasiah. This is nothing you haven't done dozens of times."

"Yeah." He turned to open the door, but stopped. "Be careful Maya."

"I will."

He stepped out of his cabin, but his stomach was in knots. He didn't like all this subterfuge and nastiness. He stalked across the common area, towards the covered area where Reece, Cole, and the rest of his inner council sat at the table chatting.

"Hey, everyone. Are you ready for this evening?"

Cole nodded. "Nothing for us to worry about."

Reece and the others nodded in agreement.

"Okay. Is Adam also taking some time to chat with the community this evening?"

Cole shrugged. "We offered him some time, but he was non-committal."

"Okay." Jasiah saw community members making their way to the common area. Cole stood quickly, "I'll get the fire going."

Cole stepped into the community area with an armload of wood. He stacked it in the firepit and began starting a fire. Jasiah saw the door to his parents' cabin open, and his mom stepped out. She walked toward him and he met her halfway.

"Is everything alright, Mom?"

"It is. There's no change in him. But, I'm going to leave the cabin door open so we can hear you. Your father wants to hear you address the community."

"I'll go in and talk to him before we start."

He kissed his mom on the cheek and walked with his arm around her shoulders to their cabin.

He stepped inside his childhood home, and felt that

sense of family and comfort he always felt here. His father was lying in bed, but his eyes were open.

"Hey, Dad. Mom said you want to hear me address the community."

His father's voice was frail, but he responded. "I do. Yes."

He took his father's hands in his and looked into his faded blue eyes. "Dad. I met someone. I'd like for you to meet her."

His mom's hand rested on his shoulder.

His dad nodded. Jasiah picked his phone from his back pocket and texted Maya. It was slow, and frustrating. Especially when he thought how quickly she could do this. But, when he tapped send, he felt a sense of accomplishment.

"She'll be here in a minute."

Softly his father asked, "Can you help me sit up? I don't want to meet your girl lying down."

Jasiah stood and moved to the front of the bed. Sliding his arms under his father's frail body, he lifted him up and his mom tucked pillows behind his father's back.

Jasiah settled him gently back, and his dad smiled.

A soft knock sounded on the door and Jasiah smiled. "I'll let her in."

He eagerly walked to the door and opened it to see Maya's sweet smile.

He kissed her lips softly. "Come in."

Taking her hand, he pulled her to the back of the cabin to meet his parents. He'd never formally introduced his parents to someone special. Then again, they knew everyone up here.

"Mom, Dad, this is Maya Sager. You met her a couple of days ago, but things have changed now. Maya, my father, Gerard Weston and my mother, Liliana Weston."

Maya took his father's left hand in hers and squeezed.

She smiled a bright smile and he saw his father's eyes come to life. "It's so nice to meet you, Mr. Weston."

She turned to his mom, and started to hold her hand out, but his mom wrapped her in a big hug. When his mom let her go, she smiled brightly. "It's nice to see you, Mrs. Weston."

"Lili. I'm Lili."

"It's nice to see you again, Lili." Jasiah pulled two kitchen chairs to the bedside and both Maya and his mom sat in them, he took up the spot at the edge of the bed and once again took his father's hand.

His father grinned. "I knew it would have to be someone strong to catch Jasiah. You're one of the special operatives from town. You're perfect."

Maya laughed. "I'd like you to remind him over and over how perfect I am."

Jasiah leaned forward and kissed her forehead. "I already know that."

She stared into his eyes, a smile on her face, and he knew his heart was captured. Fully, wonderfully captured.

A knock sounded on the door and Reece poked his head inside. "I'm sorry to bother you folks, but Jasiah, it's time."

He heaved out a deep breath and squeezed his dad's hand. "I'll stop back later to get your take on my comments."

His dad smiled. "You'll do wonderfully."

His dad's eyes swept to Maya. He nodded, "Thank you."

Her smile grew. "Thank you."

They both hugged his mom, and he took her hand and led her from the cabin and to the common area where the community had gathered.

They brought their kitchen chairs or benches they'd made over time and found a spot around the fire.

He kissed Maya as he reached the area where he'd be

addressing his community and there were some sighs, and some gasps. But, by now they all knew. Not much got by up here.

He whispered, "Be safe."

She smiled brightly. "Give 'em what you got, Jasiah."

She walked toward her brother, who stood to Jasiah's right at the edge of the woods.

Jasiah turned to his community and nodded.

"Thank you all for coming. Tonight I stand before you, excited, humble, and eager to be your president. But not because of my birthright. I want to be your president because you want me to be your president. It's just that simple."

Applause sounded and he waited. It was hard not to turn and look for Maya.

"I want to share what plans I'm making for our community. What wonders we can create up here for ourselves. I've spoken to Mayor Rayleigh Winters of Glen Hollow, and he's welcoming anyone up here who'd like to start a business to do so. It's simply a matter of filling out an application. Your business will be your own. I know Coup wants to start a woodworking business and Elle wants to start a sewing shop. You're both welcome to do that. We can build stores up here, over on the west ridge, where tourists will come and buy your wares. We've brought water and electricity and gas. Houses are being converted every day. We will need to reconfigure our common area here, so we have more parking. And, we can live our lives as we always have, in peace. But this peace is a true peace. No fighting with the town below. No worries about how we'll make a living. Jobs are being gained every day. We now have more than thirty percent of our community working. That's phenomenal."

Mr. Winger, one of the elders, stood up, "And how are

you getting paid? Are we going to have to pay a portion of our paychecks to you?"

Jasiah smiled. "I'm glad you asked that. The mayor has set aside funds from the tax rolls to pay for the president's position. He's also set funds aside to add a police officer up here so we don't have to wait so long for assistance. There are other things we've been discussing to help us out up here."

His heartbeat began to slow, his community was behind him. What he saw when he looked at his people were smiles. He turned to see his mom standing in the doorway to the cabin and she smiled and nodded. He wanted to see Maya, but she was hidden in the woods.

"And what about the shooting? Do we have to worry about any more criminals coming up here and shooting people?"

[illegible] cation of [illegible] He sounded

Her comm unit clicked. "Maya, Tate just called. The thumb drive held video of King talking to Senator Jackson about the murder in Yerezdan. He admitted to the fact he'd sent men over to shut the Chief of Staff of Yerezdan up. He admitted to the arms for oil deals. He's on video and audio."

"Wow. [illegible] Have there been any danger on the cameras?"

"Negative."

Her heart beat faster. It was almost over. They had the proof. The senator withheld that little nugget in case he needed it. Leaving it with a little girl, likely hoping it would get to the right person. She whispered, "Good on you, senator."

Her comm unit clicked again, it was Tate. "Listen up. I have Adam Jacobs on camera right now speaking to someone in a car with Tennessee license plates."

"That's Jasiah's opposition in this election," she hurried.

"Roger that."

She turned toward the common area, Jasiah needed to get to safety.

Tate spoke once again. "The car is headed up Second Road."

Maya replied. "Where's Adam Jacobs?"

"He's driving up First Road."

"Myles, Spencer, Jasiah is closest to First Road."

Maya was on the opposite side of the perimeter. She'd ducked into the woods so she wouldn't be a distraction. The revving engine of a car speeding up the road sounded and she exited the woods across the common area. She ran as fast as she could toward Jasiah. He didn't seem to notice her as he answered questions.

She saw Spencer exit the woods between First and Second Roads. He ran toward the vehicle speeding to the top.

Adam Jacobs raced on foot from First Road toward Jasiah. Spencer trained his weapon on Adam, but held. Maya yelled, "Jasiah."

Adam ran straight toward Jasiah and jumped on him from behind. There were too many people in the way. She couldn't stop him from getting to Jasiah. Myles ran toward Jasiah from the opposite side as Adam Jacobs. From the corner of her eye she saw Spencer wrestling with a man he pulled from a vehicle. People scattered in all different directions. Chairs flew back as people stood quickly and ran. Myles took two steps and jumped to pull Adam from Jasiah.

Her heart was in her throat. She felt like she was in slow motion. Her feet didn't seem to work properly and she couldn't fill her lungs completely.

She approached Myles, Jasiah, and Adam. Myles held

Adam's arms behind him, his eyes trained on Jasiah. She ran to Jasiah. "Let's go."

"Go where?"

Taking his hand, she tugged him toward her Jeep.

"I'm not leaving."

"The hell you aren't."

He stood firmly, she was no match for his size. Maybe she could match him in stubbornness, but not size.

"Tate, I can't get Jasiah to leave."

"Take him to his cabin." Tate ordered.

She stopped and faced Jasiah. "Please. Please at least go to your cabin. I can't assess the threat right now and you need to be safe."

"They all need to be safe."

"They are. Please."

His shoulders dropped slightly as he turned and jogged toward his cabin. She followed him closely. As soon as he entered the cabin she spoke to her teammates. "Jasiah is in his cabin."

Myles spoke next. "I have Jacobs hog-tied and Spencer just hog-tied the assailant from Tennessee."

Maya looked at Jasiah. He stood at the window watching what was happening. "Jasiah, you shouldn't be in the window. If someone wanted to shoot you, they'd have an easy time of it."

"Maya. We can't do this. Not like this. It makes me look weak."

"It doesn't. It's keeping you safe."

"A leader who runs isn't a leader."

"A leader who's dead can't lead." She squared off. Face-to-face they stood. His fists were balled up, his chest heaved.

Tate came over the comm unit. "Report in."

She listened as her teammates reported in. She waited until last. "Maya Sager. Safe."

Tate spoke again. "Spencer and Myles, what's the situation at this time?"

Myles responded first. "I have Jacobs secured. He keeps saying he was trying to help Jasiah. That man wanted to kill him. I don't know if I should believe him."

Spencer reported next. "I have the man from Tennessee. He isn't talking. How do you want us to transport and where?"

"Is there a place up there we can question him?"

She looked at Jasiah. He was angry. She'd never seen his jaw so tight. "Jasiah. Tate is asking if there's a building up here where we can question Adam Jacobs and the assailant from Tennessee."

Jasiah's brows bunched together. "Jacobs is in on this?"

"We don't know. He's claiming he was trying to help you."

"Fuck." He took a deep breath. "The church."

Maya responded to her teammates. "We can use the church up here. What is your assessment of Jasiah coming out of his cabin?"

She waited and stared at Jasiah while she did so. His eyes bore into hers. He was pissed. Normally when he looked at her his eyes were loving and soft. She wanted that look back on his face.

Myles responded. "I think it's safe. We've searched the perimeter. No signs of anyone else in the vicinity."

Addy chimed in. "The computers are clear. Nothing going on."

"Thank you."

"Jasiah. The area is clear. You're able to leave the cabin now. Is the church locked?"

His chest expanded as he took in a cleansing breath. "Thank you. It's not locked. I'm going out to see if I can calm everyone down."

He started to walk past her but she grabbed his hand. "Jasiah. I had to keep you safe. Do you understand? Remember when we were in the morgue and you saw Malibu Man point his gun at me? That's how I felt tonight." She swallowed; her voice lowered. "That's how I feel."

He turned to her and pulled her into his arms. Her cheek pressed against his chest, his rapid heartbeat told her the level of his anxiety. "I'm sorry." He whispered.

He kissed the top of her head, then stepped back. "I have to get out there."

She followed him out the door and to the common area. People began picking up chairs and hugging each other. Maya watched with pride as Jasiah stopped and hugged scared women. He helped pick up the chairs that had fallen over. He stopped and asked if everyone was alright. He calmed the scared. He led.

Maya helped Myles get Adam Jacobs to the church, then sat with him while Myles went out to help Spencer bring in the assailant. They were seated on opposite sides of the church. She stared daggers at both of them.

Maya stood in front of Adam Jacobs and inhaled a deep cleansing breath. "Tell me what you were about to do to Jasiah."

"I was about to save him."

"How do you mean?"

"That guy..." He jerked his head toward the assailant. "Was going to kill him."

"How do you know? Most killers don't announce their plans."

"He stopped me at the bottom of the mountain. He asked

me who the leader up in the hills was and I told him Jasiah. Then I saw two guns sitting on his front seat. I asked him why he needed to know and he said he had something that would change a nation."

"He sped off and I knew he was about to hurt Jasiah. I sped to First Road and thought I could beat him up the mountain. I tackled Jasiah so he wouldn't get shot."

Maya stared at him for a long time. She wanted to believe him, but she knew of the bad blood. Her eyes landed on Myles' eyes. He asked the Tennessee man a few questions, but got little in return. He glanced toward her. "Rafe is on his way. He can deal with this asshole."

All was ... common area. His ... to her cabin and he strode ... hugging her. She must have been worried.

He wrapped her tightly in his arms and she sobbed into his chest.

"It's okay, Mom. I'm fine. The threat has been neutralized." He held her shaking body against him, sorry she had been frightened.

His mom pulled away slightly and looked into his eyes. "He's gone, honey."

"What?" His heart sank. Dread filled him as he hurried into the cabin to see his father's body, still lying in bed, slightly propped as he'd helped him do earlier. The sheets didn't rise and fall with his breathing. His eyes were lifeless and half opened. Jasiah sat at the edge of the bed and took his father's cold hand in his. The ache that filled his heart was beyond any he'd ever felt before. He'd have to move on without the rock he'd always counted on. His mentor. His best friend.

His mother stood next to him, her hand on his shoulder. "He heard you speak. He was so proud of you. I'm proud of you." She squeezed his shoulder.

Jasiah swallowed the enormous lump in his throat and tried to focus on his breathing. The sadness that squeezed his heart wouldn't let go. His chest was so heavy he struggled to fill his lungs with air. He'd feel this loss the rest of his life.

His father wavered and moved as the tears filled his eyes. He let them spill down his cheeks. His mom pulled his head to her body and hugged him tightly. "He loved you so much Jasiah. You were the light of his life."

"I loved him so much. He was my hero." He sobbed. It felt good to let it out. Cleansing.

He let himself cry it out, then he pulled back from his mom and sniffed. "I'll miss him the rest of my life."

His mom rubbed his shoulders. "Me too."

He stared at his father for a while longer. Just one last minute with him. One last moment. He silently prayed he was no longer in pain. That he was healthy and happy once again.

With a last shudder of a breath, he stood and hugged his mom once more. Wiping the tears from his eyes, he straightened his shoulders. "I'll get Elenor to help you prepare."

"Thank you, Jasiah."

Filling his lungs with air once more, he opened the door and stepped out to a world much different than when he'd entered this cabin. He strode to Elenor's cabin, which was along the edge of the grounds between Second and Last Road. A light was on in her cabin as he stepped on the front porch. He knocked solidly on the door and within a few seconds, the door opened, and Elenor peered out at him.

"Jasiah. How can I..."

Her hand flew to her mouth and they stared at each other for long moments. Finally, Elenor whispered. "He's gone?"

Jasiah nodded but said nothing more. He wasn't sure he'd get the words from his mouth without breaking down.

"I'll run to your mother right now."

He nodded and Elenor reached out and squeezed his hand.

Swallowing the dry knot in his throat, he squeezed her hand in return. Stepping from the porch he went in search of Maya. He needed her right now.

Crossing the common area to the church, he heard voices inside as he neared. Hesitating at the door, hand on the handle, he squared his shoulders and opened the door.

Maya's eyes landed on his across the room. She instantly stood and hurried to him.

Her arms reached out to him, the concern in her eyes weakening his resolve. He pulled her outside and leaned against the wall near the door.

"Jasiah, what's wrong?"

He swallowed repeatedly before he could speak. Finally, he whispered, "My father passed."

"Oh, Jasiah. Oh, honey, I'm so sorry."

He held her close, her arms slid up his back, and squeezed him tightly. He held her close, her body's warmth pressed to him was the only place he wanted to be right now. Her scent wrapped around him, her presence was calming.

She spoke into his neck and he held her tight. "Is there anything I can do for you or your mom?"

He sucked in a deep breath. "I don't know right now, honey. I just needed to hold you close."

Her arms tightened once more and he closed his eyes.

After a few moments, he pulled back. "Thank you."

"Of course. Should I go and see if your mom needs anything?"

"That would be nice. Elenor is there with her. They'll prepare Dad for viewing tomorrow and we'll have a burial tomorrow night."

Maya stepped back and looked into his eyes. "What are you going to do?"

"I'm going to find Reece and let him know. The men will need to build a coffin. I want to take part in that. It's tradition. I'll likely be home late tonight."

"I'll be there waiting for you. Do what you need to do."

He kissed her lips softly, looked into her eyes once more, then turned to find Reece and set the wheels in motion for a funeral and burial.

He watched Maya stride across the common area to his parents' cabin, pride filled his heart. She was amazing.

Reece met him near the fire. "How are you?"

"I'm fine. We have Jacobs and the assailant in the church. The special operatives are debriefing them."

Reece nodded.

"Reece. My father passed. We'll need to build a coffin and prepare for the funeral. I need you to set things in motion for that, please."

Reece reached a hand out to him and he took it. "I'm sorry Jasiah. That's rough. He was a good man."

"He was. Thank you."

"I'll get things rolling. We'll build the coffin right next to the fire here. If you want to get the tools, I'll get the men to bring the wood."

"Thanks, Reece."

He moved to the shed where the tools were kept. It felt good to have a duty to focus on. He managed a deep breath without that squeezing pain as he opened the door to the shed. His mind went in a thousand directions, but he knew what needed to be done next and that was a start.

[illegible] and she [illegible] it was Jasiah [illegible] was strong and gracious and Maya found a new pride in this family as they prepared to bury a loved one.

[illegible] ago, and saw the men building the casket for Gerard. They worked together and it seemed symbolic and poignant. She was happy Jasiah had this group with him. She was proud once more of his strength and adherence to rituals.

Tapping her mom's photo on her phone she lifted it to her ears. "Hey, honey, how are you?"

"Hi, Mom. I needed to hear your voice."

"Oh, Maya, what's wrong?"

She inhaled a deep breath, "Jasiah's father passed away today."

"Oh, honey, I'm so sorry. Is there anything we can do?"

"Can you come here before Thanksgiving? I could sure use hugs from you guys."

"I think we can absolutely make it down there before Thanksgiving. Should we come for the funeral or after?"

"I'd appreciate it if you could come for the funeral. But, it's tomorrow."

"Oh." Her mom was silent for a moment. She heard whispering and knew she was chatting with her dad. "We'll be there tomorrow afternoon."

"Thanks, Mom. I sure do appreciate it."

"Honey. We love you so much. I can't wait to wrap my arms around you and hold you close. And, we're looking forward to meeting Jasiah."

"Same for me, Mom. Tell Dad I love him. I love you too. See you tomorrow."

"We both love you, baby girl."

The call ended and she took a deep breath. She removed her clothing and slipped into the bed, which felt impossibly large for only her. Jasiah's pillow smelled of him, that woodsy scent she'd fallen in love with. Pulling it toward her, she buried her face into his pillow, wrapped her arms around it, and fell asleep.

———

A warm husky body slid in behind her and wrapped his arms around her. She inhaled the scent of wood and witch hazel and musk. Jasiah was home.

He kissed her ear and whispered. "I love you."

"I love you too."

She snuggled into his body and relaxed.

Maya left the mountain, and her mountain man, and parked in her spot in the garage at the HOG. Her mind spun in all directions. Snapping her head to bring her focus back to the present, she took a deep breath and exited her Jeep. She entered the kitchen, and Helissa, their cook, was busily preparing breakfast.

"Good morning, Maya."

"Morning, Helissa. How are you? It smells delicious in here."

"I'm fine. Tate told me about Jasiah's father. Please accept my condolences. I'm preparing some food for you all to take up to Hickory Hills."

"Thank you so much. That's lovely."

Helissa grinned. Her graying hair was pulled back and twisted behind her head. Her brown eyes were sincere. "You're welcome. Tate is waiting for you in his office."

"Thanks, Helissa."

She stepped through the kitchen and turned left to head to Tate's office. She knocked on the partially open door and Addy opened it and gave her a big hug.

"I'm so sorry about Jasiah's father. He was a nice man."

"Thank you." She hugged Addy back and absorbed her warmth. She'd seen little of her friends and teammates here lately. That was a problem with living up on the mountain, not that she lived there, but she'd spent a fair amount of time there lately. She'd do better at getting together with them more often.

Maya whispered, "Mom and Dad are coming today."

"Oh, I can't wait to see them." Addy squeezed her again. "I have to get Rafe some coffee. I'll see you in a little while. I've missed you."

"You bet. I've missed you too."

Addy moved away from the door and strode toward the kitchen. She'd been so happy since she met Rafe. Now that Maya had met Jasiah, she understood the feeling.

Entering Tate's office, she smiled in greeting. "Good morning."

"Morning, Maya. How are you today?"

"I'm good."

"Okay. First, I'm very sorry to hear of Gerard's passing. Even though we knew it was coming, it's never easy when it happens."

"I appreciate your words. I'll let Jasiah know."

Tate nodded. He smiled softly, "Let's get to the report."

"Before we do that, can you update me on where things stand with the man from Tennessee?"

"Yes. He's in jail right now. Adam Jacobs has been released. I do believe he meant Jasiah no harm."

"Okay. He seemed sincere last night, and that was my feeling."

Tate nodded. "Okay, let's begin."

A knock sounded on his door. "Sorry, Maya. Come in."

Rafe stood at the door. "Morning. Good morning, Maya. I'm sorry to interrupt. But, Daniel King stepped away from the presidency this morning. Vice President Elect Chad Marshal will be inaugurated in his place in about eight weeks."

"Oh my God. That's fantastic news. How did they make him agree to step back?" She asked.

Rafe shrugged. "I don't have all of the facts just yet. I'll let you all know as they come in. You may want to watch the news stations as it's breaking now."

Tate nodded. "Thanks, Rafe." He stepped around his

desk and the two men hugged and did that back slap thing men do. "Great job."

"Great job by GHOST, as usual."

Tate sat at his desk once again. "Let's get these reports finished and watch the world change."

"Sounds great."

39

It had to be [illegible] to honor his father by doing the very best job he could do.

Sweat dripped from his forehead. Though it was crisp this morning, he'd put all of his energy into sanding, then rubbing this oil into the wood. He'd soon finish it off with a coat of beeswax [illegible].

Elenor approached and admired the finish. "You do such great work, Jasiah. Your parents are rightly proud."

He stood and stretched his back. "Thank you, Elenor. The least I can do is have something beautiful to lay him to rest in."

Elenor's lips parted in a soft smile. Her hand rested on his forearm. "You've done that."

He stared into her eyes. "Thank you. It means a lot to hear that."

She nodded once. "We have him prepared and ready."

His shoulders slumped. While he'd been working meticulously on this casket, he'd managed to believe he was making something his father would love. That fact came crashing down hearing Elenor say the words, prepared and ready.

He nodded as his throat clogged with emotion. He repeatedly swallowed to get his emotions in check, but she seemed to understand and nodded before moving on.

Stepping back, he stared at the casket. This side only had a few more inches of stain to apply, then he'd complete it by rubbing the beeswax in. He blew out a loud breath, dipped his rag into the stain and continued rubbing it into his father's resting vessel.

His mind flipped back and forth between his father and Maya. One was his past, one his future. He needed to focus on his future. His future looked bright. He'd waited long enough to find her. Maya. He'd be an old dad, at least an older dad. He was already forty-two. But, he wanted kids badly. That was something he'd never thought of all these years, not until he'd met her.

His phone rang and it took him a few rings before he realized what it was. Carrying a phone around was still rather new to him.

"Jasiah Weston."

A sweet giggle reached his ears and the grin on his face came naturally.

"Maya Sager."

He chuckled. "I was just thinking about you."

"Oh, I hope good thoughts."

"Always."

She was silent for a moment. "I missed you and wondered how you're doing. Are you doing okay, Jasiah?"

Tears hit his eyes so quickly it caught him off guard. He sniffed slightly. "I'm alright. I'm about to begin rubbing beeswax into the casket. Then, it'll be ready for him. I'll get ready then and we'll be down the mountain by noon. The funeral is at one. I can't wait to see you."

"I'll be at the funeral home at noon to be with you and your mom while final preparations are made. Helissa is making food for us to bring up afterwards. My entire team will be there. My parents are coming also."

His heart twisted slightly. "Wow." He sat on a bench left over from the melee last night. Someone would claim it later. His breathing became choppy. Taking in a deep breath, he let it out. "Your support and that of your team and parents is overwhelming. Thank you."

She tsked. "Of course, I support you. I'm with you. Always."

He swallowed profusely. "I'm always with you, baby."

"Anything I can do? How is your mom?"

"Elenor and the other ladies have been with her this morning. They have him prepared for burial. They've prayed. They've visited. She's been busy, which is good. Tomorrow will be different."

"Yeah."

He sat up straight. "Are you staying with me tonight?"

"Yes."

A smile formed on his lips. "Great. I can't wait."

"I'll see you in a couple of hours. I love you."

He chuckled. His future looked pretty damned good. "I love you too, baby."

He heard her giggle before the call ended and his heart felt full.

He picked up the pot of beeswax and started applying it to finish the casket. His final gift to his father.

———

J asiah's eyes searched the parking lot for Maya's Jeep. He felt a hot pit in his stomach when he didn't see it. He'd thought of her for the past few hours and couldn't wait to hold her hand or wrap his arm around her. Swallowing his disappointment, he stepped from his truck and hurried around to open the passenger door for his mom. She smiled at him as he helped her from the truck. Her dark dress and hat made her face seem paler than usual. Lack of sleep and extreme loss such as this didn't help.

He walked beside his mom as they entered the funeral home. It was the first time his community had a funeral in town. All of this was new and not exactly a happy occasion.

The instant the door closed, the room was dark. He heard his mom gasp, and he laid his hand on her shoulder. "Let your eyes adjust, Mom." He whispered.

Soon his eyes grew accustomed to the dimness of the room, and he managed to look around. A beautiful woman stood with two people near the doorway of another room. She turned to face him and her smile, that gorgeous familiar smile, greeted him. Maya's hair billowed around her shoulders in curls. She wore something shiny on her lips and something made her lashes longer and darker. Quite simply, she was stunning.

She moved toward them and he grinned. She wore dressy shoes with a slight heel on them. Not her customary combat boots. Her dress slacks hung delicately over her legs and the soft pink sweater made him want to squeeze her tightly like a stuffed animal.

He stepped forward and pulled her to his body. He buried his nose in the crook of her neck and inhaled her scent. Citrus, clean, soft and powdery. All good things.

"Thank you for being here."

She chuckled into the crook of his neck, "I wouldn't be anywhere else."

"I didn't see your Jeep outside and I worried."

She pulled back and looked into his eyes. "I rode with my parents."

She turned and held her hand out to her parents. He pulled his mom forward.

"Jasiah and Lili, I'd like to introduce you to my parents. Dodge and Jax Sager."

Her mom, who could have been Maya's twin looked into his eyes. "I'm very sorry for your loss, Jasiah. But, I'm happy to meet you." She hugged him softly and he choked up.

He heard her father greeting his mother, then turned to meet the man who was so important to Maya.

He held his large hand out and Jasiah took it solidly and squeezed tightly. "It's nice to meet you, Mr. Sager."

"Dodge." He pumped a few times. "It's nice to meet you, Jasiah."

A man in a suit approached them. "We have the room ready for you. The family only first, then we'll let others inside."

Jasiah nodded and looked at his mother. She nodded once and he turned to the Sagers. "Please join us." He put his arm around Maya. "You're family."

[illegible] Adam Jacobs
[illegible] stepped closer to Jasiah.
[illegible] the smile valiant. Adam

Adam held his hand out to Jasiah. "I'm deeply sorry for your loss. Gerard will be missed."

[illegible] Adam. I appreciate it."

Zara nodded, but didn't move to hug him. Marni's sad eyes glanced up at Jasiah, and he knelt down so he could look into her eyes easier. "I'm sorry. I liked Mr. Gerard."

Jasiah grinned and nodded. "He liked you too, Marni."

Her eyes rounded and a smile formed on her lips. "Really?"

"Really."

She looked over to Maya and Maya stepped closer and knelt down. "I'm sorry for you too, Maya."

Maya smiled a big bright smile. "Thank you, Marni. And

thank you for all of your help in catching a bad guy. We did it."

Marni's smile grew so large her eyes disappeared. Zara placed a hand on Marni's shoulder and the little girl turned and walked away with her parents.

Maya looked into Jasiah's eyes. "She's cute."

He leaned closer, "Not as cute as our babies will be."

Her heartbeat raced. "I love the way that sounds."

Lili approached. "We're cleaning up now. People have wood to get in for the night and chores to do. Please make up plates to take home. We have so much food."

They prepared plates as Jasiah walked them to the cabin as the women pitched in to clean up. Men tended the fire, cleaned up the leftover wood from this morning, and told stories about Gerard. Her parents said goodbye to Lili and others. Then hugged Jasiah. Finally, her mom squeezed her tightly. "I like him. He's special and good for you."

"Thanks, Mom." She squeezed her mom tightly. "You and Dad stay in my room. The others will be floating in this week to stay for Thanksgiving. I'll come down every day to visit. You're always welcome to come up here."

Her mom chuckled. "Believe me, we came this far, I'll be visiting with my baby girl."

"Don't hog her, Jax. I get some time too." Her dad chuckled. He scooped her up in his arms and squeezed her tightly. She'd always loved his hugs. "I love you, Daddy."

"I love you too, baby girl."

He kissed her cheek and set her on the ground. He leaned over and shook Jasiah's hand and grinned. "You treat her right."

"It's my honor to do so."

They got in their vehicles and she watched them drive away. Jasiah wrapped his arm around her shoulders and pulled her close. They waited until the last of the vehicles disappeared down the mountain, then he tugged her. "Let's go home."

She swallowed as they moved toward his cabin. She was incredibly tired at this point. It had been a lot of emotion today. But, she and her teammates had met all of the people who still lived up in Hickory Hills and she felt more confident than ever that Jasiah was the leader they needed. Her heart felt full.

———

Maya woke to voices outside of the cabin and the sounds of logs dropping on the ground. She rolled over to see Jasiah's side of the bed empty. Stretching, she slid from the bed, dressed quickly, and giggled when she saw a coffee cup on the counter next to a nearly full pot of coffee.

She pulled a heavy sweater over her long-sleeved t-shirt and stepped out of the cabin to visit the outhouse. Jasiah stood with a group of men, they were discussing building something and pointing to the logs. He turned to see her and grinned.

"Hang on, guys."

He hustled toward her. "I'm glad you're awake. I have a surprise for you."

"A surprise? What kind of surprise?"

He chuckled and wrapped his brawny arm around her shoulders. Leading her to the side of the cabin he pointed to grooves drawn in the ground. It doubled the size of the cabin.

"So, this will be a larger kitchen and a bathroom. Complete with shower - for shower sex," he chuckled.

"And, showers."

"Right. Yes, but shower sex too. I can't wait."

She laughed. "So, you'll have a toilet, sink, and shower in here?"

He nodded. "And, a place for a refrigerator, stove, and more counter space. Where the table is now in front of the fireplace, we'll buy a sofa like you have down below. We don't have anything like that now, so we can sit on the sofa in front of the fire."

Emotion clogged her throat and her nose tingled. Her eyes watered and the side of the cabin wavered from the tears in her eyes. "That's beautiful, Jasiah."

"I want you to have everything. It's going to be loud and messy for a couple of days, but before Thanksgiving, we'll have a larger cabin."

She turned and faced him. "That's wonderful, Jasiah."

He grinned. "And, I have one more thing."

He took her hand and led her to the woods. He turned and followed a path into the woods. "Do you recognize this place?"

She glanced around the area, then noticed the thicket of brush in front of her. "This is where we hid from Malibu Man when he killed the senator."

"This is where I met the woman of my dreams. She came to me through that entrance over there. I waved you over and took your hand urging you to kneel down. And I watched you chase him and couldn't have been more impressed by you. Tiny little woman with big confidence and bravery."

Her heart began to race. Pride blossomed again as she watched his face. Staring into his eyes, her love grew stronger than she believed it could. She swallowed emotion, she focused on breathing evenly. She was failing at even breathing.

He knelt down on one knee. "Maya Sager. Helen of Troy. Baby. Will you marry me?"

A sob tore from her throat, it came deep from inside her chest. She opened her mouth but words wouldn't come. She finally swallowed and took in a deep breath. "Yes." It came out as a whisper, but she'd say it louder as soon as she could speak again.

He pulled a ring from his shirt pocket. A thick gold band glinted in the light that shown through the trees. Both edges of the band looked like lace, a thin shiny gold ring circled the center. He slipped it on her finger and she stared at it. It was exquisite. And perfect.

"My mother has made jewelry for years. She'd been working on this one for a long time and hoped one day I'd give it to the woman of my dreams. She gave it to me yesterday. I see it fits perfectly, so I believe, it was meant to be. On the day we marry, a thin gold band will fit tightly with the lace and have a ring of diamonds in the center."

"Oh my god. Jasiah." She was breathless. "It's simply perfect."

He stood and she threw her arms around his shoulders and planted her lips against his. His arms circled her body and held her closely. When they parted for air, she tucked her nose into the crook of his neck and kissed him. Her eyes closed tightly and they stood together for a long time. Her life changed the second she'd entered these woods not long ago. She never would have guessed.

41

____

[illegible] today [illegible] _wedding Day._ And the [illegible] would be completed by making Maya his wife. He wanted to marry today because he couldn't ever be more thankful than he'd be on the day he married. At long last, he was going to be married.

Maya's mom insisted she spend the night in Glen Hollow last night citing some bad luck wives' tale about seeing the bride before the wedding. He spent the night finishing up the shower. A plumber came from town the past couple of days and worked on the installation of the sink, toilet, and shower. He hooked up the kitchen sink, and the refrigerator had a water spigot in the door, which he hooked up. He laughed when he walked around the cabin. The size had doubled, the conveniences were amazing. The only thing they needed was a sofa. He wanted Maya to pick it out.

A knock on the door called his attention, and he opened it up to find his mom standing before him.

He reached down and hugged her close. "Good morning. Would you like to try a cup of coffee?"

She smiled. "I would."

He spent a bit of time explaining the coffee pot to her, then handed her a fresh cup of coffee. "If it's bitter, you can add cream or sugar or both."

She sipped and winced. He chuckled. "Creamer?"

She nodded and he pulled the powdered creamer from a cabinet and sprinkled it in her coffee, it disappeared and turned her coffee a lighter shade of brown. She sipped again and smiled. "That's pretty good."

He chuckled. "Let me show you around."

"Watch this." He pulled a glass from the cupboard and held it against the water dispenser in the refrigerator door. Water poured out and she gasped. "Well, I'll be."

He laughed. "It's pretty great."

He showed her the stove and she whispered, "Wow."

Then he showed her the bathroom. She was filled with wonder at it all and he saw pride in her face. "You've done a beautiful job with all of this Jasiah."

"I'll do it for you too, Mom. We can have it finished in a couple of weeks. Before Christmas we can have the addition built and the appliances installed."

"Let me think about it."

He laughed. "Fair enough."

She pulled a handkerchief from her deerskin coat pocket. "I finished this last night. I think it turned out stunningly well."

She unwrapped Maya's wedding band. The scalloped edge would fit tightly to the lace edge on her engagement ring. The diamonds wrapped all around the band, so no matter which way she looked at it, it would sparkle.

"It's gorgeous, Mom." He kissed her temple and stared at the ring he'd put on his bride in a couple of hours.

"Also, the residents are lining up to vote."

"Thanks, Mom. Did you vote yet?"

She smiled. "I'm going right now, then I'll bathe and get ready for your wedding. I just wish I had the time to make a proper wedding cake."

He hugged her. "Maya wanted pumpkin pie. Traditional Thanksgiving. We're so blessed, this will be perfect."

Her lips curved up in a smile. "I'm so happy for you, Jasiah."

"Thanks, Mom."

She waved her hand around. "I'm going to vote for my son to be president."

He laughed as she left his cabin, a beautiful smile on her face.

Jasiah stared at the wedding band for a long time. Heaving out a deep breath, he turned to bathe and get ready for today.

———

Tires crunching on the road caught his attention. He'd been sitting on the back porch, looking out over the mountains and valley below. Tomorrow he and his bride would have a cup of coffee together as the first day of the rest of their lives began.

He stepped into the cabin, checked his tie in the mirror, smoothed his hair and took a deep breath. He stepped onto the front porch and surveyed the area as the cars parked. They'd all come up here and he was proud they'd all be here to celebrate all today brought.

He sauntered across the common area, which had been

transformed with something called, dinghy lights. One of the women found them in town and was so excited as the men hung them on poles. They crisscrossed the common area, lighting it up as the sun went down. He saw Jax exit a vehicle as Dodge held her arm. She smiled up at Dodge and he kissed her lips. Jasiah smiled as he watched them.

Dodge then moved to the back of the SUV and opened the door. Maya stepped out looking more than stunning. She was absolutely the most beautiful woman in the world. Her dark hair shone in the lights, it billowed out around her shoulders in curls. Her white dress billowed out like a cloud of soft material, and stopped at her calves. She wore white heels which made her look taller. Her shoulders were exposed, and the dress crossed between her breasts in a 'V' shape. She was absolutely exquisite.

His mom came to stand next to him. She gasped. "My goodness she's stunning."

"I agree."

Maya's smile was radiant as she slowly walked toward him. Her eyes never left his. She carried a bouquet of white roses and the gold band on her left hand glinted in the lights.

She stood before him, radiant and smiling, and the breath left his body.

He finally managed to say, "You are perfection."

She laughed. "I was going to say the same about you. I've never seen you in a tie."

People assembled around the common area, and Pastor Richards stepped forward and asked, "Are you ready?"

"Yes." His voice cracked, but he nodded to confirm. He cleared his throat, "Yes."

Maya laughed. "Yes. I'm ready."

They said their vows before family and friends. He made

Maya his wife, and he couldn't remember a day he'd ever been happier. The rings on her finger glittered all night. Every time he glanced at her, she smiled brighter.

The food was plentiful, they bowed their heads as Paster Richards said the prayer before they ate and they celebrated.

At seven p.m. Reece stood up and tapped his fork to his glass. "We have the election results."

A shiver ran down his spine, and Maya leaned over and whispered. "I'm so proud of you."

"I haven't won yet."

"It doesn't matter."

He kissed her lips, heard a couple of 'awes" then turned his attention to Reece.

"Fifty-one votes for Jasiah Weston. Four votes for Adam Jacobs. Our president is Jasiah Weston."

Maya's arms flew around his shoulders and her lips pressed tightly to his. "Congratulations." She said between kisses.

He stared into her eyes for a few moments, then turned to his mom who sat at a table in front of them. She had tears streaming down her cheeks and her hands clapped together in unison with the rest of the group.

Someone yelled, "Speech. Speech."

He smiled at Maya and stood. He held a glass of cider in his hand and waited for the applause to die down.

Swallowing the emotion he felt, he took a deep breath. "If any one of you would have told me a few weeks ago how much my life would change, I would have thought you had found some elixir and downed the entire bottle."

The crowd laughed. He swallowed and looked at his bride. "I've been unreasonably blessed this year. I've suffered heartache too. But, I'm excited for all that lies ahead of us here in Hickory Hills and I promise to work tirelessly for the improvement of our lives up here. I promise to always do my best for all of you."

Applause once again sounded, and he waited. He bent down and helped Maya stand up. He wrapped his arm around her waist and after the applause stopped he took a deep breath. "I'm proud to stand before you, side by side with my bride, and agree to be your leader."

He kissed his wife's luscious lips then whispered. "I love you."

She laughed. "I love you too."

[illegible] about this over

"And you're sure about this?"

"I am. It makes perfect sense. When this one joins us..." She pointed to her still flat stomach. "I want to be close. We need law enforcement up in the hills and I'm the most qualified. It solves a couple of issues."

Tate smiled and shook his head. "I never would have believed you'd be pregnant before Addy. To be honest, before Spencer, Henry, or Myles."

Maya laughed. "To be clear, Spencer, Henry, and Myles can't get pregnant."

He laughed out loud and she laughed with him. "*Touché.* You know what I mean."

"I do. I can't believe it either."

"You know you can come back anytime you want? I mean it. And, if you ever crave a bit of action, we'll likely have something for you here."

"Thanks, Tate."

Maya stood and walked around his desk. She hugged Tate. Her childhood friend and playmate turned boss. But, he was always her friend.

She exited his office and crossed the living area to Rafe's office. She knocked on the door.

"Come in."

She opened the door to see Rafe sitting at his desk, computer screens lined across the wall above him.

"Hey, Maya. How are you?"

"I'm good. Do you know where Addy is? I looked for her earlier but didn't see her."

"She's out at Henry's today. Everleigh has another colt being born and Addy wanted to see it."

"That's fantastic. I'm heading out there to see it myself."

The HOG was empty today. It made her feel rather sad. She'd hoped to come in and see everyone, but she hadn't called.

Exiting the HOG she jumped in her Jeep, backed from her parking spot and drove down the road. She passed the farm fields and homes that dotted the area she'd fallen in love with after living here for a couple of years.

She turned right and drove to Henry and Everleigh's farm. As she pulled into the driveway, she saw all of their vehicles. Myles, Spencer, Addy, and Lara's SUV was there and so was Kenna's. She hopped down from her Jeep and strode into the barn. Addy turned to see her first and ran over to hug her. "I'm so happy to see you."

She squeezed her cousin, fresh back from her honeymoon. "I'm happy to see you too."

Addy grabbed her hand and pulled her toward the stall they all stood around. Myles reached over and wrapped an arm around her shoulders and kissed the top of her head. "Hey, sis. How are you?"

"I'm good."

It was dark in the barn, and her eyes took a moment to adjust. Spencer and Kenna stood at one end of the stall, eagerly watching the colt soon to be born. Everleigh and Henry were in the stall with the horse. Henry made a good farmer. Everleigh did too. She'd done a tremendous job with these horses.

Henry glanced at her and stood. He reached over the stall and hugged her. "Hey there. You good?"

"I am. How about you?"

He beamed. "We're good. This is number four for us."

"That's fantastic, Henry."

Everleigh turned to see her and waved. She knelt by the mare's head and offered words of support.

Spencer looked down the rail line and waved, so did Kenna.

Lara entered the barn, with another person and as soon as Maya heard her voice she knew it was Lara's best friend, Shianne. Shianne was a nice gal, owned her own clothing boutique and made it a go even in such a small town. She'd mastered the online sales game and that's where most of her money came from. But, that girl could talk your ear off.

Lara waved at her and hugged her. "Hey. How are you? I just spoke to Tate." She whispered.

Maya whispered back, "I'm good. I haven't said anything yet."

"Okay."

Shianne waved. "Hi, Maya. Nice to see you."

"It's nice to see you too, Shianne."

Then, Maya's heart fluttered. Shianne looked at Myles, and her face turned pink. She softened her voice, "Hi, Myles."

Myles turned and smiled at Shianne. "Hey, there. How are you?"

"Good."

Shianne moved to stand next to Myles and Maya had this funny feeling in her tummy that something was brewing there.

Movement in the stall captured her attention and Addy gasped. "Oh my god. Here it comes."

They stood in silence as the momma mare, pushed and grunted and pushed until her foal came tumbling out. Henry reached over and pulled the foal away.

"Ev, honey get ready for her to stand." He called out.

Everleigh stood and moved to the foal. She took a rag and wiped at its nose and mouth so it could breathe. The mare struggled slightly, her legs and hooves floundered around until she found footing and she stood. Her legs shook and she waited until she'd gained her strength, then she turned around and began licking her foal clean.

Henry pulled Everleigh to him and kissed her lips. "Congratulations, Ev. We have a boy."

They embraced as everyone clapped and cheered for Henry and Everleigh's new foal. Their farm had started making good money. These horses they'd adopted had been pedigreed and their foals made the farm nice sums.

Her friends then high-fived each other and Henry and Everleigh.

Everleigh wiped her hands on a clean rag. "Let's let mama take care of her baby in peace. I've got drinks in the house for everyone."

Lara added, "I have cookies."

As a group they walked and chatted and it felt like old times, with some great additions to their group. Inside the house, Everleigh went to the washroom and washed her hands. She stepped out and said, "Help yourselves in the kitchen, I'm going to change clothes."

Lara laid a box of cookies on the table and Maya reached into the refrigerator and pulled out a pitcher of lemonade. Kenna pulled glasses from the cupboard and they filled their glasses and ate cookies. It was a much lighter celebration than they'd all had in years past. But, it was perfect just the same. They were missing Aidyn and Tate, but they were always in contact.

Maya noticed Shianne standing close to Myles and he laughed and chatted with her. Addy moved close to her. "How are things in the hills, Maya?"

"Things are good. Jasiah is busy every day and we just hired a police officer to work up there, so we're moving forward."

"Really, who did you hire as a police officer?"

Maya grinned. "Me."

Everyone stopped talking and stared at her as if she'd sprouted another head.

Myles straightened his shoulders, "Say again."

Maya smiled at her brother. "I just came from talking to Tate. I won't be an operative with GHOST anymore, I'm going to work up in the hills as their police officer."

Myles' brows bunched. "Why?"

Maya took a deep breath. "Because in about seven months I'm having a baby and I want to be close to him or her after he or she is born. Jasiah's mom will take care of him while we both need to work, but I don't want to be out of town on a mission for long periods."

Myles stalked toward her, his eyes locked on hers. "I'm going to be an uncle?"

"Yes."

"Oh my god." He wrapped her in his arms and pulled her close. "Oh my god. That's so exciting."

He stepped back slightly, and Addy wrapped her in a warm embrace. "Congratulations, cousin. I'm so happy for you."

"Thank you, Addy."

Spencer and Kenna congratulated her with hugs, then Henry and Everleigh. Henry's cheeks turned pink when he cleared his throat. "I don't want to steal Maya's good news, but join in with it. Everleigh and I are going to be parents at about the same time. Maya, I hope our children will play together like you and I did as kids."

Maya hugged Henry tightly. "I hope so too, Henry."

Kenna laughed and Spencer nodded. "Us too. Six months."

They congratulated each other on their impending children and the only thing that could have made it better was Jasiah standing here with her. But, she'd share this moment with him.

Maya waited for a lull. "Since we all have so much to celebrate, I'd like to invite you all up to the hills and let's have a party to celebrate all of our babies, our good fortune, and our friendships."

Maya hopped from her Jeep, pulled the bags of goodies she'd picked up while in town and grinned all the way to the cabin. Opening the door she stepped inside to a blazing fire and her handsome husband sitting at the table with papers strewn out around him.

"Hi. What's all this?" She motioned to the papers.

He smiled but stood and took the bags from her.

"Applications for the line of businesses we're building on the ledge. Mayor Winters calls it a strip mall. Our residents don't like the sound of that, so I'm trying to come up with a better name for it."

"Ahh. Yeah, it's not really a strip mall. There will be, what? Four little shops?"

"Yeah. Four."

She shrugged. "What about The Shoppes on the Hill. Or The Shoppes in the Hills?"

Jasiah laughed. "I'll toss those out to the committee."

He kissed her lips then glanced at the bags she'd brought in. "What's all of this?"

"Ah, well, I bought Marni some cute colored bottles I found in the flower shop in town. And, I couldn't help it. I bought this." She reached into a bag and pulled out a cute yellow baby onesie.

Holding it up for him to see it said, "Daddy's little hunting buddy."

Jasiah's eyes welled with tears as he stared at it. He swallowed, then nodded.

He pulled her to his body and hugged her tight. He whispered, "I can't wait."

Maya squeezed him to her tightly. He smelled musky and earthy and fantastic. But, she smelled barn on her sleeve.

"I should take a shower, I smell like a barn. Oh, Henry and Everleigh had a boy today. And, they're having a baby around the same time as us. And, Spencer and Kenna are having one a month before us."

Jasiah smiled. "You'll need to tell me all of that later. I stopped listening when you said you needed to take a shower. I need one too, we finished mom's cabin retrofit today."

Maya's lips spread across her face. "Are you thinking what I'm thinking?"

Jasiah took her hand and tugged her toward the bathroom. "I'm way ahead of you."

What's going on between Myles and Shianne? You can bet it's going to be fun! Find out here - https://geni.us/Shianne-All

If you prefer to follow my newsletter for all the release information, stories about my life and sales, follow me here - https://geni.us/PJFialaNL

ACKNOWLEDGMENTS

Throughout writing the GHOST Legacy series, I've asked my Road Queens to name characters, places, and businesses. They've responded with wonderful names! Below are all the contributions to the GHOST Legacy characters, places and businesses and the lovely readers who were so creative and generous to have named them.

The file became so large, I had to move it to my website. Simply click the link here - - https://www.pjfiala.com/ghost-legacy-acknowledgements/ to read all the names, businesses and places associated with GHOST Legacy.

ALSO BY PJ FIALA

You can find all of my books at https://pjfiala.com/books

Romantic Suspense

Rolling Thunder Series

Moving to Love, Book 1

Moving to Hope, Book 2

Moving to Forever, Book 3

Moving to Desire, Book 4

Moving to You, Book 5

Moving On, Book 6

Rolling Thunder Boxset 1, Books 1-3

Rolling Thunder Boxset 2, Books 4-6

Military Romantic Suspense

Second Chances Series

Designing Samantha's Love, Book 1

Securing Kiera's Love, Book 2

Bluegrass Security Series

Heart Thief, Book One

Finish Line, Book Two

Lethal Love, Book Three

Wrenched Fate, Book Four

Lynyrd Station Protectors - Security

Finding His Fire Book One

Finding His Mark Book Two

Finding His Jewel Book Three

Finding His Match Book Four

Big 3 Security Boxset, Books 1-3

Lynyrd Station Protectors - Special Ops

Defending Keirnan, LSP Special Ops Book One

Defending Sophie, LSP Special Ops Book Two

Defending Roxanne, LSP Special Ops Book Three

Defending Yvette, LSP Special Ops BookFour

Defending Bridget, LSP Special Ops Book Five

Defending Isabella, LSP Special Ops Book Six

LSP Special Ops Box Set One (Books 1-3)

LSP Special Ops Box Set Two (Books 4-6)

Lynyrd Station Protectors - Trafficking

RAPTOR Rising - Prequel

Saving Shelby, LSP Trafficking Book One

Holding Hadleigh, LSP Trafficking Book Two

Craving Charlesia, LSP Trafficking Book Three

Promising Piper, LSP Trafficking Book Four

Missing Mia, LSP Trafficking Book Five

Believing Becca, LSP Trafficking Book Six

Keeping Kori, LSP Trafficking Book Seven

Healing Hope, LSP Trafficking Book Eight

Engaging Emersyn, LSP Trafficking Book Nine

LSP Trafficking Box Set 1

LSP Trafficking Box Set 2

LSP Trafficking Box Set 3

GHOST Legacy (Next generation)

Finding Lara, Book One

Saving Elena, Book Two

Rescuing Kenna, Book Three

Protecting Everleigh, Book Four

Guarding Adelaide, Book Five

Shielding Maya, Book Six

Blossom Springs Series

Servicemen of Blossom Springs

Steamy Nights

Sultry Nights

Seductive Nights

MEET PJ

Writing has been a desire my whole life. Once I found the courage to write, life changed for me in the most profound way. Bringing stories to readers that I'd enjoy reading and creating characters that are flawed, but lovable is such a joy.

When not writing, I'm with my family doing something fun. My husband, Gene, and I are bikers and enjoy riding to new locations, meeting new people and generally enjoying this fabulous country we live in.

I come from a family of veterans. My grandfather, father, brother, two sons, and one daughter-in-law are all veterans. Needless to say, I am proud to be an American and proud of the service my amazing family has given.

My online home is https://www.pjfiala.com.
You can connect with me on Facebook: https://www.facebook.com/PJFiala1,
Instagram: https://www.Instagram.com/PJFiala
Tiktok: https://www.tiktok.com/@pjfiala?lang=en .
If you prefer to email, go ahead, I'll respond - pjfiala@pjfiala.com.

COPYRIGHT

Copyright © 2023 by PJ Fiala

All rights reserved. This book or any portion thereof may not be reproduced or used in any manner whatsoever without the express written permission of the publisher except for the use of brief quotations in a book review.

Publisher's note: This is a work of fiction. Names, characters, places, and incidents either are the product of the author's imagination or are used fictitiously. Any resemblance to actual events, locales, or persons, living or dead, is entirely coincidental.

Printed in the United States of America
First published 2023
Fiala, PJ
SHIELDING MAYA / PJ Fiala
p. cm.
1. Romance—Fiction. 2. Romance—Suspense. 3. Romance - Military
I. Title – SHIELDING MAYA
ISBN-13: 978-1-959386-12-4